Diabolical Dreamscapes

First published in 2023 by Leilanie Stewart

Diabolical Dreamscapes Copyright © 2023 Leilanie Stewart

Cover and internal artwork Copyright © 2023 Leilanie Stewart

ISBN: 9781739952372

Thank you for supporting independent publishing.

Website: www.leilaniestewart.com
F: facebook.com/leilaniestewartauthor
Twitter: @leilaniestewart
Instagram: @leilaniestewartauthor

Diabolical Dreamscapes
Strange and Macabre Short Stories

Leilanie Stewart

To Joe and KJ, who are always with me on the road less travelled.

CONTENTS

Part 1: Dark and Surreal Tales of Death

Elsie's Eternal Eden

Elsie dug deep into the soil with her trowel, her wrinkled hand turning white with her grip on the handle. The potato was starting to come loose. She wedged the trowel in further and it popped up in a shower of earth, along with several strands of black hair.

Her eyes widened behind her large spectacles. Transfixed, she pulled on a clump of hair, bringing up a scrap of grey-green skin attached to it.

She shook the hair from her hand and looked down at the potato, which was full and round, about the size of a cantaloupe. The tuber had been feeding on the decaying remains the whole time.

Elsie thought back to when she planted the potato seeds in late May. And she had moved into the house in March. So the person - probably a woman, judging by the long hair, had been buried since before then. But fairly recently, since there was still some flesh remaining. Maybe it was the body of the previous owner; though why would someone be buried in their back garden? She hadn't heard anything about a murder or strange disappearance in town. It was a peaceful, suburban neighbourhood.

She shrugged. "Oh well, no point letting my potatoes go to waste," she said aloud, then hummed *Tip-toe through the Tulips* as she harvested the rest. The song was perfect as it stopped her from thinking. Perhaps picking potatoes to eat from someone's grave wasn't the most respectful thing to do.

As she shuffled back indoors, Elsie admired the batch of potatoes in her arms. Each one was large and round, bigger than what her outstretched palm could hold at any one time. If her cabbages and carrots were to grow super-sized in the same way, she would be able to enter them into the Guinness World Records, or, at any rate, display them at the town's vegetable show.

"One of these will make enough mashed potato for three nights' worth of dinners," she mused to herself, picking out one of the largest. She piled the rest into a moth-eaten hessian sack in her basement pantry and pulled the drawstring tight.

Dinner that night was a feast. Elsie said grace over her meal of cottage pie and mixed vegetables with a verse from her King James Bible, carefully selected to remind her that eating from the natural earth was in no way wrong. She cleared her throat in preparation to recite Genesis 3 verse 19:

"In the sweat of thy face, thou shalt eat bread, til thou return unto the ground; for out of it wast thou taken: for dust thou art, and unto dust shalt thou return."

After a breath, she continued. "Thank you, dear woman in the backyard, for lending the compounds of your flesh to the nutrients of my meal."

Elsie looked through the conservatory window at the back lawn, blue-green in the twilight. She scooped a spoonful of buttered mash and minced beef into her mouth, and closed her eyes as the rich taste swirled over her tongue. Once her meal was finished, she hobbled into the kitchen to do the washing up, feeling tired and full.

She was flipping through the TV guide, ready to settle down for the evening, when she heard a thud from downstairs. She opened the pantry door and switched on the light. The single bulb threw a bright glow over the bare wooden staircase. One of the potatoes had rolled into the middle of the concrete floor. Elsie raised her eyebrows. Must have popped out of the bag somehow. It was a moth-eaten bag, after all.

She switched the light off. The potato could lie there. It had simply singled itself out for her next meal.

As she lay in bed content that night, Elsie heard a bang.

"Blast," she said, wincing. "I must have stacked the pile too high and collapsed the lot. They'll be all over the floor by tomorrow."

***

Elsie enjoyed her tea and toast in the bright morning sunlight of her conservatory, and decided to check her potatoes before doing more gardening, although there had been no more noises.

The cool air washed over her as she opened the pantry door. She turned on the light and gasped. The concrete floor was bare.

In the far corner, a figure stood no higher than her hip. The hessian bag was a bulging torso, pinched at the top by its drawstring into a bunch. Its legs were of large misshapen spuds. The arms were a chain of smaller potatoes, which had sprouted at the ends to form gnarled fingers. Who could have made such a thing, and why?

"It must be the little people helping out," she muttered, "I could use it as a scarecrow, especially to keep the birds away from my vegetables." But how would she get it up the stairs?

Elsie stooped to grab the hessian bag. She managed a firm grip on both corners, preparing to lift it, when its hand closed around her wrist. Staggering backwards, she let out a startled scream.

She clapped a hand over her mouth. Stars swam before her eyes, and she willed herself not to pass out.

"Who are you? What do you want?" she asked.

"I'm the keeper of your garden," said the creature, using its hands to work the drawstring, opening and closing the mouth of the bag as it spoke. "I'm the watchman of your soul," it said in its gravelly voice.

Elsie licked her lips, her mouth dry. "Did the little people send you?"

The watchman shook. "You grew me. Did you forget so soon?"

She closed her eyes, her heart racing. Such a creature had to be unholy, surely? "This is unnatural."

"Come, I'll show you," it said.

She inched up the stairs. The watchman moved towards her on its stumpy legs, making a thud with each step. Its hessian body twisted as it climbed behind her, sliding potatoes about inside with a dull rustle. The drawstring swung across its torso like a pendulum, touching each arm. She kept creeping backwards, not taking her eyes off it, until they passed through the French-doors of her conservatory and into the back garden.

"Look all around you," said the watchman.

Elsie's eyes travelled over bushes, flowers, shrubs. Sprigs of colour erupted into clouds of butterflies. Flowery vines twisted their way up overgrown fences. Fruit trees shivered in the cool late summer breeze.

"It's your own little slice of Eden," said the watchman "And for those who came before you. It lends itself to you, then you lend back. Life goes on in this way."

The watchman pointed a rooty hand towards her vegetable patch, where grey-green human fingers sprouted erect among the leafy carrot tops, and tufts of black hair served to ward off rabbits and deer with the scent of humankind.

"She was a keen gardener too, the one before you," said the watchman. "Now, come this way."

Elsie followed her guide towards the end of the garden, where a young lemon tree stood, its fruit still immature. The watchman pushed the branches aside to show its woody trunk. She looked closely and her jaw dropped. A baby's face was captured in the wood, like a sleeping angel carved into the very essence of the plant.

"The fairies took him when his mother went," said the watchman. "This is his shrine, which will stand forever in Eden."

A wave of fear swept over her. She understood.

"...Thou shalt eat bread, til thou return to the earth..."

The watchman was nodding. "Yes, you have tried manna from this slice of heaven and now it is your turn to give back. I'm here to collect your payment so the ones who come next may thrive."

She shook her head and tried to back away, but found that her feet were rooted to the ground. Deep inside, she could feel a seed germinating, a root pushing its way out. From the crown of her head, a single leaf floated to the ground and she knew that the autumn of her days had come. Soon winter would set in. And in the spring, the fruits of a new life would blossom.

The London Plane

Gladys put both hands on the tree and pulled herself up from the ground. She could see the waning moon through the bare branches. The sky was indigo blue, her favourite colour. The great artist had painted it all for her. She felt it.

"I was here before. I touched this tree once."

Once, under a tranquil sky.

Her knees were still bleeding. She could see grit and fragments of leaves stuck to the grazed flesh. There was nothing she could do for now. More important things mattered. Like finding out how to get home.

She could feel the bark cracked and dry beneath her splayed fingers. As she stepped back, she let go of the trunk and looked at the medley of colours; brown, red, yellow like flax. There was a tree exactly like it outside her apartment back in England. A London Plane. A beautiful tree. Her favourite. She loved how they shed their outer bark in layers to reveal a multitude of colours beneath. A divine way to rid themselves of pollution.

Impulse overcame her. Her fingers worked like pale crabs, scuttling across the woody surface, peeling flakes from the tree. Fresh bark showed underneath the dead dregs of autumn. Around the trunk she walked, tearing at the tree. As the last flake of old fell, impulse gave way to addiction. Slivers of new green growth fell atop the pile of dead bark.

The trunk became thinner as she worked and Gladys noticed too that it was changing shape. As she peeled, the branches fell around her, exposing the nakedness of the moon. The tree was now a stump of its former self, standing barely five inches above her height. She pulled from the top, ripping lignin strands like threads of celery, until a dome appeared. Running her hands over the smooth surface following the line of the wood, she saw two distinct broad mounds, like shoulders. Yes, the shape she had carved was definitely human. Male.

Carved? Or revealed?

Her nimble fingers set to work again. The fresh bark was still wet. Digging her fingers into the dome, she opened a hole. Forcing more fingers in, she grabbed enough to fold back the wood. Underneath, she saw skin. A cheek. An eye, closed. Black hair, short and curly.

A man's head came into view. His head fell limp against his chest, lolling on his collarbone.

"Hello? Are you alive?"

Gladys touched his face with her green-stained fingertips. The man didn't respond. She felt his neck. There was a faint pulse. Placing a finger under his nose, she felt warm air rush over her hand.

I have to get him out, she thought. She tore at the bark, ripping chunks off from his chest, down his torso until finally his legs and feet were free. The man slumped to the ground and lay over the tree shavings, his arms outstretched.

"Wake up. Mister?"

She shook his shoulders gently and his head flopped back, making his mouth open. Tapping his cheek with her palm didn't work either.

Could he be diabetic? She fumbled inside his shirt pocket and her hand closed around a small bottle. Reading the front, she saw the words 'Temazepam' written on the front.

Instinct. She felt his chest. No heartbeat.

"Oh God. Warren, wake up."

Warren? Gladys felt a jolt in her chest. How could she possibly have known his name? She had never met him before.

Tilting his head back, she saw his Adam's apple protrude. She pinched his nose with her thumb and forefinger and blew two breaths into his open mouth. Making a fist with her right hand on his chest, she pushed on it with the left. Twenty seven. Twenty eight. Twenty nine. Thirty.

Again, two breaths. She sensed him move and sat up.

"Gladys. My angel."

His blue eyes were bright indigo, reflecting the sky above. A tear rolled down Gladys' cheek and fell onto his.

But why was she crying? Over a total stranger?

"You saved my life," said Warren, pushing himself up. He propped himself up on both elbows.

"You took an overdose," she said, wiping her wet face.

"Thank you. I'd be dead if you weren't here."

She helped him to his feet and he dusted off fragments of wood.

"Do you know where we are?" said Gladys.

"I'm not sure, but I know this place from the back of my mind somewhere," Warren said. He scratched his ear. "I can't think when I was here before though."

"Do you know me?" she said.

"Yeah, I think so. But again, I don't know how."

"I know you too. I'm sure I met you in another place once."

He smiled. "A dream?"

She shook her head. "No. Another place. Back in London, I think. I'm not sure if I'll ever be able to go back there. I'm trying to find my way home."

"Me too. I think I know where to go."

He took her hand. They climbed down off the pile of wood and walked across the dry earth under the watch of the moon. The sky hadn't changed at all. It wasn't any darker. Although the moon was brighter. Gladys stared up at it. She knew time had passed.

They were on a flat plane, the ground veined with cracks. The desert was vast. Gladys could see distant mountains, purple under the evening sky. Warren was taking her towards them. She looked back. The remains of the only tree that had graced the arid land lay like the mound of a fresh burial.

"Why were you in that tree?" she asked.

Warren looked at her, his eyes darting between hers as he searched her face.

"I don't know. But it was something to do with you, I think."

"With me?"

He shrugged. "Maybe I was there for you to find me."

They continued, bare soil passing under their feet as miles came and went. The mountains drew closer. Gladys could see a fissure in the rock forming a passageway, and knew he was taking her towards it.

"Warren, I'm scared. Do you think it's a good idea to go in there? Can't we go around?"

"It's safe. Do you trust me?"

She nodded and squeezed his hand.

Shadow fell over them. The sky above was obliterated. Darkness crowded them, like a cloak. All Gladys could feel was the touch of his hand. Where was the moon when she needed it? No moon, no sky. No air.

Her throat felt constricted. Was she holding her breath in the tenseness of the black passage? She tried to call out to Warren, but had lost her voice.

The pain in her throat was growing in the darkness. Without air, she was suffocating.

Help. Help, she thought but knew he couldn't hear. No one could.

She was going to die if they didn't get out of the passage soon. Could they turn back? If she ran, she would make it. She could go around the mountains as she had suggested.

And then a pulse in her forehead, carrying with it a thought. A memory. Of a past life.

Warren please. Don't do this. Stop.

Her tongue was protruding now, scouring the dark space for air. But there was nothing in the void apart from his hand and her.

You made me do it. It's all your fault. You make me get angry, you bitch!

Her eyeballs were pounding. Her head felt like a pustule, ready to burst. The pressure was too much. She needed release.

Ahead, she saw a slice of blue. The sky. The beautiful sky. Her feet carried her forwards and the moon was waiting to welcome her, like a mother with open arms to her child.

Gladys inhaled, drinking in a rush of cool, soothing air. Warren turned and smiled at her.

"Everything is going to be alright now."

Gladys clutched at her throat and felt rough skin around her jugular. She felt a loose piece hanging and picked it off. The flake of dried blood was burnt umber like the bark on the London Plane. Nails had done it, hands that had intended her harm.

But it couldn't have been Warren. He had been holding her hand the whole time, leading her through the blackness. Only a memory. But it had been so real.

"We're nearly there now," he said, squeezing her hand.

Wasn't he alarmed by her injuries? Had he not noticed? Again she looked to the moon for advice, but it hung above her like an innocent bystander.

Gladys didn't turn back again. She wanted to forget the mountains falling behind her. One thought alone filled her mind. Home.

As they walked, a towering rock came into sight, like a dark pillar silhouetted against the twilight sky. Warren pointed ahead at it.

"That's where we have to go."

Gladys looked at it and her hand fell away from her throat. She lifted her chin and walked forward.

But as she looked closer at Warren, she could see blood.

Yes, there was definitely blood on the back of his head. The drops were falling behind him like a trail. She could see an open cut, an inch long laceration.

"Warren, stop. You're bleeding. The bottle cut you badly."

As before, she felt a jolt in her chest. How did she know?

She just did. The details were trickling back to her, clearer on this side of the mountain. Green glass shattering over cranium, the pieces falling through depth and mist as she lay amidst a magnesium stearate rain.

He stopped and walked back to her.

"It's okay." He held her face in both hands and wiped across her cheeks with both thumbs. "We've both made mistakes."

"What?" she said, pushing off his hands. "What do you mean?"

Looking down, she saw blood on his fingers.

Her eyes were pouring red tears. Like radioactive fallout, they dripped over her clothes.

"Let's keep going. There's still time. We'll make it home," said Warren.

The rock pillar was looming ever closer and on it, Gladys could make out a white spot. Closer still, a circle. Closer. A clock.

Thirty feet. A distant siren.

Twenty feet. A wailing war cry.

Ten feet. The Grim Reaper was knocking.

They were there. Warren smiled as he placed his hand on the hour hand of the clock and turned it back. And Gladys smiled with him.

Til Death do us Boneapart

Bastet lay on the floor. She didn't recall how she had got there. Nor did she know why there was broken glass all around her. All she knew was that she was entirely wrapped, from neck to foot, in swaddling. She tried to move, but her front legs were strapped tight along the front of her body. She wanted to kick out with her powerful hind legs, but they too were tied down. What about her tail? Could she manoeuvre it enough to pierce a hole in the bandages?

No. There was nothing for it. She would have to summon her Divine powers. What was the use in being a cat deity, if she couldn't work some magic? Fair enough, she had her current bondage to contend with, but she had to try something.

Hold on; it was all coming back to her now. A dry, sandy place. A sealed room where she had lain in darkness for what felt like an eternity. A man, young and handsome and bold. Loving hands placed her in... in... Yes. She remembered clear as day. A wooden crate. Then? A rocking motion and the sound of the sea. A strange noise followed; a whirr and groan, unfamiliar to her, accompanied by an incessant chugging motion. Smoke, lots of choking fumes. Next, a glass case. Faces, different from those in Egypt. Not beautiful and brown, but round and white. Curious. A strange language. And now? In another crate, more wood. Another glass case, more faces, a new language.

She remembered. It had been a long time. No, an eon. By Ra, had it been that long? Yes. And the truth of the situation? She had to face the awful truth. Not only was she a cat, but she was mummified.

But how had she contracted amnesia, and furthermore, why had she chosen this moment to awaken?

Bastct looked around. The shattered glass came from the display case in which she had stood gathering dust. She had fallen from her pedestal onto the museum floor and by some quirk of fate she was now free.

Willpower! If it wasn't to be magic, then she would motivate herself upright by thought. Bastet concentrated hard and felt herself lift, until she balanced on her bandaged rump. Wonderful. And now to see if willpower would propel her forward.

Yes. Bastet bounced towards the exit of the Egyptian Antiquities department. She slipped easily through it and rolled down the stairs.

***

The night air blew around Bastet, cool and keen. She was grateful she hadn't encountered a museum guard along the way. It helped to be a cat in the shadows. She found she could stray into a dark corner much more easily than one of the human mummies might have managed.

First things first. The whole episode had unnerved her. She needed a smoke. Ahead, light emanated from a single dwelling on the dark street. She bounced closer to it and saw that it was a shop of some kind. Perhaps the seller would have lotus for her. Or even mandrake. At such a late hour, henbane too might suffice.

Bastet breezed through the automatic door. She bounded up to the counter and launched herself onto a crisps rack in front of the till. The teller looked to be a dozy sort of teenager, lank and spotty, reading a book. He was either sleep-deprived or drunk to look that way in the early hours of the morning.

"Hello," said Bastet. "I wondered what you have in the way of smokables."

"Dis en francais?" said the boy.

"What?" Bastet asked.

Of course, she was in France. She'd spent the last six months in the Louvre. Not enough time to pick up the blasted lingo, unlike her decade-long stint in the British Museum. There, she'd picked up English from the janitor who liked to talk to himself in the early mornings. He smoked Benson and Hedges too. Wonder if they had them in France?

"Benson and Hedges," she said. Hopefully the simplified language would help her in her current predicament. The boy looked quite stupid.

He blinked at her. "Identification, s'il vous plait," he said. He jabbed a finger at a picture of an I.D. badge.

"Look here, I am over eighteen. Eighteen hundred is nearer to the mark, but still a long way off. Now give me cigarettes please, as I am gasping for a puff!"

"Je ne peux pas le faire," said the kid, in a monotonous voice.

"Pour quoi… that is to say, why not?" said Bastet, trying to speak in her Louvre-learned French.

"Parce que. Tu es fait de matière sèches. Si tu prends feu, c'est ma responsabilité. Maintenant, pars."

Bastet translated quickly in her head. "Listen to me, boy, I've managed to stay intact since eight hundred BC. I don't think one cigarette will do me any harm."

The boy smirked. "Cela me fera du mal, cela pesera sur ma conscience."

So he understood English all along! "Listen, I have nothing to lose. I'll hardly die of lung cancer. And if you don't give me the cigarettes, I shall bounce behind you and take them off the shelf. If it is a fight you want, so be it!"

The kid shook his greasy head. "Ce travail de nuit me prend vraiment la tête," he mumbled. "Alright then, here you are," he said in heavily-accented English. He punched a few buttons on the cash register.

Oh no! Bastet had forgotten; how would she pay?

"If you want to pay by card, there'll be an extra two Euro charge. You got that *Monsieur*?"

Bastet puffed up. "Mister? I will have you know that I am a female feline. You will address me as madam. Have you got that clear?"

The kid blinked at her, then scratched his head. "Whatever. I'd just really rather not be shouted at by some sort of… of night terror."

"Night terror? Well, I've never!" Bastet snatched up the cigarettes. "For your audacity alone, I shall take an insult-fee. I will have these smokables for no cost. Consider them paid by ass-hole tax. Good night to you, sir!"

She bounced off the counter, turned and made for the door.

***

It had taken Bastet until dawn to unwrap the cellophane box and nudge out the first cigarette with her bandaged muzzle. She had manoeuvred the long item into her mouth by pushing the orange end against the ground. Fortunately, a passing drunk had given her a light, without paying too much attention to having a mummified cat for a passing companion. Bastet had continued smoking the rest of the pack by lighting each cigarette in turn and now felt sufficiently satisfied of her craving. Night came and went. Bastet leaned against a tree, puffing on her cigarette. Pity she couldn't taste it, but she could imagine it all the same. She inhaled, smoke filling her dried body, pushing the bandages until they strained. What a delirium of pleasure. What decadent delight, of which she had been deprived for nearly three millennia.

Nephthys, her mistress in Egypt, had mostly smoked lotus, occasionally mandrake. Bastet had lounged by her owner, inhaling the dizzying eddy of fragrant fumes. When Nephthys had passed on into the afterlife, East of Abydos, Bastet too had left the world of the living. She had been sacrificed, wrapped tight and placed in a temple at Bubastis as an offering to the cat deity. How she had longed for more lotus leaf, but had been met only with the scented air of incense in the temple.

Bastet was quite distracted by thoughts of the past, when a woman came along the street walking her dog. Before she had time to snap to her senses, Bastet had been lifted and held high for inspection.

"What's this we have here?" The woman spoke English. "Looks like those robbers have been hitting the Louvre again. Oh well. One more for my collection."

The dog, a little white Westie, began barking at Bastet and straining against his leash.

"Necromancer, that's enough! This one isn't a live cat, you can't chase her, you silly dog!"

The woman tucked Bastet under her arm and continued on down the street, her dog trotting by her side. Bastet was only starting to think what fate would befall her, when they turned a corner into a narrow street full of town houses.

Her new home. The woman placed Bastet on a velvet cushion on what looked to be an antique sofa. She'd seen such furniture in the Louvre and in the British Museum, when they'd moved her from one wing to another. It had been her one chance to see the other exhibits before she'd been stored in her glass cabinet. Those days of being scrutinised, admired by hundreds every day were over. Her new place of residence seemed to be a spacious apartment filled with antiques. Bastet felt relieved that there was no sign of the woman's dog. Maybe it stayed in another room. Dogs could be a menace to cats, children too; or at least the wicked ones, like those who grabbed her tail and swung her into the Nile. Did the woman have a family? Perhaps she lived alone. Bastet's thoughts flitted onwards to a logical conclusion; would life get boring in a private household?

The woman came into the room with a tray full of biscuits and tea. Bastet watched bewildered through a slit in her bandages, as a cup was set before her. The English were into their tea, sure, but wasn't this a bit extreme?

"Now then kitty, would you like to join me for some English breakfast?" The woman held the steaming tea to Bastet's mouth. Was this some sort of eccentric British tea party? Bastet decided she would oblige her kind host and indulge herself. She let her bandages soak a drop of moisture, enjoying the liquid on her parched lips.

"I wonder what I shall call you?" The woman stared out the window, her eyes glazed. "You must have belonged to an ancient Egyptian princess, or even to the great Pharoah Seti the First himself. Why else would you have been so lovingly mummified?"

"Bastet," she purred. "My name's Bastet."

The woman didn't hear her. "I've got it… the perfect name. I'll call you Neith. The great mother of the Egyptians and goddess of the home. You shall be keeper of my home while I go out on my daily errands, or to take my dog, Necromancer, for a walk. You will become Neith, the guardian of my apartment."

***

Bastet sighed with contentment. She had everything a mummified cat could ask for. Her body had been adorned with a beautiful, multi-coloured, hand-knitted vest. Her owner was a compassionate woman. The normal humdrum that she would otherwise have succumbed to away from a stimulating museum was filled with soothing music and the fascinating chat of her host.

"Now then, my darling Neith, I shall leave Mozart playing for you while I go to the morning market. I must have my cheese and tomatoes fresh to go along with my coffee. But don't despair. My housekeeper Claire shall be by to clean while I am away, so you shall have a companion."

The lovely woman of the house leaned forward and kissed Bastet on her muzzle before she left the room. Bastet heard her voice carry from outside the door. "Necromancer, let's go!"

The front door slammed. Bastet snuggled back in her velvet cushion and let the music fill her heart, soothe her mind.

This was certainly a good way to spend one of her nine lives, as the English liked to put it, yet a niggle of discontentment arose. Could it be that she was simply spoiled, made ungrateful by all the kindness she had been shown? No, it couldn't be. She longed for more out of life. She ached for the old ways, lusted for what she had once had. Egypt. How long had it been?

Bastet thought hard. The archaeologist who had taken her from her tomb; what was his name? She concentrated hard despite the dust in her mind. She had lain in Bubastis for eons, entombed in the darkness, forgotten by the world of sunshine above.

She had almost resigned herself to permanent sleep when the blackness shattered; rock had shattered. She'd heard banging. Men had come with tools: hammers, picks. The men were like none she had seen before. They wore unfamiliar clothing. No beautiful gold jewellery or loin cloths, no decorative designs painted on their bodies. No white temple garments, no incense, no prayers. These people wore camel-coloured garments and strange hats. They had fair skin. They spoke in a foreign tongue. With horror, Bastet realised she was emerging into an alien world; a different age on earth, probably with new gods, a new language and an unfamiliar way of life. Firm, capable hands held her high against daylight for the first time in nearly three millennia. She had looked on the face of her discoverer. A young man, bold and handsome with strong features and dark, soulful eyes. Bastet had fallen in love. She had never known men, having been raised by her mistress, Nephthys, and surrounded by only priestesses at Bubastis. She had never known how it felt to be touched, held in a gentle, masculine grasp.

Marcel Dupree. Yes, that was his name. The adventurer, the explorer who had taken her to France in a crate and sold her on to the British Museum. She longed to see her handsome capturer once again, to be held lovingly in his arms. Being caressed by her current owner had reawakened her to the past. Perhaps if she could find Marcel, they could once again go sailing off together to the Old Country.

***

Bastet had been alone and absorbed in her fantasies of archaeological adventure for some time, when the door opened awakening her sensibilities.

"It must be Claire," she said aloud.

"Bonjour? Madame Wilson?"

Yes, it was the housekeeper, Claire. She was a French woman; maybe she would know where to find Marcel Dupree, one of her countrymen.

Better to let her know right away that she was alive, rather than give the poor girl a fright halfway through cleaning and make her break something.

"Hello," said Bastet, in a bright voice. "I don't speak much French. Can you speak English? My owner has gone out shopping."

Claire stared at Bastet, her hand over her chest. She didn't scream. Nor did she speak or move.

"I'm sorry. I hope I didn't frighten you?"

"You," said Claire in heavily-accented English. "You are a ghost?"

"No, just a cat. But not an ordinary one. I'm an Ancient Egyptian mummified cat."

"This is some sort of black magic?" said the girl in heavily-accented English. "My boss is mad... mad. This place is cursed. I always told her these idols she collects have evil spirits in them."

"I'm not evil," said Bastet. "I'm lonely."

"Does Madame Wilson speak with you?"

"Not so far," said Bastet. "She talks to me and seems to answer for me too. I never have a chance to reply."

Claire sneered. "I always told that foolish English witch she was playing with fire, collecting antiques and naming her dog 'Necromancer'."

"He's a Westie; he's harmless."

"That's what you think." Claire pointed at Bastet. "And what's that awful garment you're wearing?"

"Madame Wilson knitted it for me."

"Hmph." Claire turned up her nose. "She wastes too much time on you with her ridiculous tea parties. You're spoiled. Teacher's pet. You're like Joseph in his multicoloured dream-coat."

"Huh?"

Claire ignored her. "And do you know what happened to Joseph?"

"Joseph who?"

"Joseph from the bible. You should know, you Egyptians were cruel to the Hebrews, horrible to them."

"What happened to Joseph?"

"He was thrown down a well by his brothers, sold as a slave to your masters. And you will be punished too." Claire snatched Bastet off her velvet cushion in a one-handed grip. Bastet felt the girl's fingers dig into her body.

"Careful with me please," Bastet whined. "I'm not as agile as I once was – I might fall to dust if you carry on like this."

Claire threw Bastet down by the front door. "While I'm on shift, you're going to learn your place. No pampering for you this morning, evil creature. You'll be a draft excluder."

Bastet lay, humiliated, as Claire cleaned and hoovered. The wicked girl brought the noisy dust-eater close and rammed it against Bastet's body. Bastet had been familiar with dust-eaters from the British Museum as the janitor swept them around, and she had rather enjoyed the buzzing noise, which lulled her into a gentle sleep. But this thing was not an innocuous gadget; she could see the harm they were capable of inflicting. Her bandaged body was buffeted to and fro as the nasty girl caused her to suffer.

"Please desist," said Bastet in a feeble voice.

"You are in France. You will speak French if I am to listen. You will cry Mercy. Now beg!"

"Mercy!" Bastet cried. "Mercy, mercy…"

The wicked girl laughed. "You're lucky Madame Wilson will be back soon or else I'd have put you in the bin."

Bastet felt herself roughly snatched up and forced onto the sofa. Her woollen vest was ruffled back into shape by deft, but malicious fingers and her velvet cushion punched to plump it up.

"Take this you nasty little devil."

Claire sprayed a foul-smelling liquid onto Bastet. She grabbed a bundle of money left for her on the table and slammed the front door on her way out. Bastet trembled. Not much she could do now, but wait for her mistress to come home.

**

Could Madame Wilson really be that wise a person, if she couldn't see through such a nasty piece of work as Claire? Naivety at her age was disturbing. Madame Wilson was eccentric. Eccentricity was the next level of denial. A sort of carefree limbo; a false start of induced happiness. Perhaps eccentrics were able to block out a negative presence in their lives. Bastet thought of her own situation. She wasn't judging, so much as reflecting on her own circumstances. She'd been in limbo for three thousand years. She missed her original mistress, the beautiful Nephthys, Chantress of Amun.

Bastet sat forward with a start. Could there be any chance, however slim, that Nephthys was still in Egypt, living an afterlife in bandaged limbo too? Was there any way she could get herself back to Bubastis to find out? But how? She could bounce, that wasn't an issue, but how would she get out of Madame Wilson's flat? Stripping off her bandages by herself was impossible. It had been hard enough to manoeuvre a cigarette into her parched mouth, never mind direct a knife upwards to cut through her bonds. She'd be more likely to hack through her torso if she performed such a precarious task. Even if she could remove the bandages, how would she unlock the front door to escape?

No, no, no; it wouldn't do. She would have to wait for Madame Wilson to take her out. Only that way could she track down Marcel Dupree. She would find her handsome adventurer and he would take her off on a ship to the old world. From there, they would travel along the Nile until they reached Bubastis. A quiver of excitement swept through her arid body. There might even be a chance that Marcel would fall in love with beautiful Nephthys and the three of them would spend infinity together: the happy couple and their loving pet.

Yes; she had a mission. The willpower surged through her torso as a physical force, propelling her forward. Bastet tumbled off the velvet sofa and landed on the plush rug with a soft thud. A hand reached around her midriff and Bastet felt herself lifted up.

"Oh, my lovely Neith, what have you been up to while I was away?"

Bastet looked into the caring eyes of her Mistress, Madam Wilson. Sadness welled. Her journey had been quenched before it had even begun.

Necromancer, the little Westie, came into the room. He placed himself between his owner's legs, pulled back his lips and growled at Bastet.

"Necromancer, how did you get out of the bedroom, you silly dog." Madame Wilson hushed the dog, but he didn't stop. Being confronted by two rows of carnivorous white teeth made Bastet sick to her leathery core.

"I said stop that growling." Madame Wilson pushed Necromancer and he left the room with a rejected whine.

Close shave. Bastet wanted to sigh with relief, but couldn't find the air. Madame Wilson held her up to eye level. A curious expression overcame Bastet's mistress as she looked at her. Bastet wasn't sure if it was bewilderment or intrigue. She inserted a finger into the gap in Bastet's bandages at eye level and widened the peep hole. Madame Wilson's eyes widened.

"Oh my! Wonderful Neith, powerful Neith – I couldn't believe it at first, but I felt it with my own hands. You quivered. I saw the glint in your eyes – you're alive!"

***

"Talk to me, oh ancient one."

Bastet looked at the candle-lit face of Madame Wilson across the Ouija board. The candles around the edges flickered in an other-worldly breeze.

"Are you a spirit inhabiting the body of this cat?"

Bastet looked at the Ouija board. Nobody from beyond was present with them. She herself wasn't dead, having never entered the netherworld East of

Abydos. Madame Wilson moved the indicator to the word 'yes'.

"No," Bastet shouted.

Madame Wilson yelped and knocked over a candle as she jumped up. She patted the flame out with her hands and peered up at Bastet from the carpet.

"There is no spirit, only me," said Bastet.

"You – you can talk," Madame Wilson whimpered.

"Of course I can talk."

"Why didn't you talk to me sooner? I've had you for over a week."

Bastet thought for a moment. "I tried a few times, but you were having such fun pampering me and answering for me and calling me Neith. I liked being loved. Besides, I was worried that if you knew I could talk, you might make a sideshow attraction of me."

Madame Wilson shook her head. "Oh, dear me, I would never subject you to such a thing. You're special, and you came into my care. I've wanted this all my life."

"What – to talk to a mummified cat?"

"No, my darling, to contact a deity. To learn of the ancient wisdom that has been lost."

Bastet tried to think of what ancient wisdom she had. She knew about cleaning herself and coughing up hairballs. She knew how to catch mice and bring home birds for her mistress Nephthys. "I'm not a deity, I'm a common housecat that happened to live in Bubastis. I got my name, Bastet, after the holy offering place."

"Bastet? But I summoned you from the Afterlife, therefore you must be a goddess?"

Bastet tried to shake her head, but her neck was rigid. "Afraid not. I'm a humble pet looking for her old mistress and the way back to my homeland."

"Your mistress? You mean, there's another Ancient Egyptian around here somewhere?" Madame Wilson looked excited.

"No, she resides in Bubastis where she was a Chantress of Amun. She took care of me at the temple. When she died of a disease of the water, I was sacrificed as an offering to the goddess Bast. We were both mummified and placed in the temple. But we were separated, and I was left to the ravages of time."

"Do you mean to say you want me to take you back to Egypt?" Madame Wilson looked more composed, though her voice remained shaky.

"I wouldn't ask that of you. There is another way. The man who brought me to France and sold me on to England was an adventurer called Marcel Dupree. I need to find him."

"Marcel Dupree? Do you mean the eminent archaeologist and explorer?"

Bastet fought to suppress a tremor of excitement. "You know him?"

"I know where his remains are, yes. He died a long time ago, before the turn of last century. They buried him in a cemetery outside of Paris, but when they had housing problems in the sixties and expanded into the suburbs, they dug up the graveyard and moved all the bodies. He's part of a display now over at the catacombs."

"Could you take me over there, please?"

"Of course, Bastet my love. But I should warn you, he's not in an able-bodied state. It might be hard for him to do anything. That is, supposing he even exists the way you do. I doubt there's any Ancient Egyptian magic keeping him alive."

Fear gripped Bastet. "Why might it be hard for him to do anything?"

"Because he's only a skull. His cranium was used as part of a heart-shaped decoration, along with hundreds, thousands of other intellectuals, artists and commoners. They're all equal now – a massive unknown in the ethereal world."

Bastet jittered. "Then how do you know which skull he is? And can you find the rest of him?"

"My forays in the occult led me to him, along with certain, shall I say, connections at the museum."

Bastet's patience had been exhausted. "Connections? Why didn't you say so earlier? Do you know any archaeologists who might help?"

Madame Wilson blushed. "No. But I've had associations with the right kind of men to amass my particular collection of antiques. How do you think I keep myself in comfort without a job?"

A memory flooded back to Bastet's mind; scantily clad women scouring the markets for men, taking them behind the stalls to do their business in exchange for a piece of gold. Clearly Madame Wilson was better at her trade if she could live in a luxurious Parisian townhouse.

"Well, now that we know where the other is coming from, could we please go to Marcel Dupree? I don't care if we can't acquire the rest of him, his head is the important part. He can direct us back to my mistress Nephthys."

Madame Wilson folded up her Ouija board, but left the candles burning. "Alright then. Tomorrow we shall go graverobbing. But for now, we have a lot to catch up on. I want to hear all about your old life in Egypt. It sounds so romantic."

***

Bastet spent an anxious night fretting about the intricacies of the job. Did Madame Wilson have the necessary tools? A pick, like those Hebrew slaves used to build the great pyramids? And how would they avoid being seen? Madame Wilson at least, seemed to have the same issues on her mind. She was up and dressed at the crack of dawn.

"Good morning, my darling Bastet. I hope you enjoyed some rest overnight?"

"Some. I don't sleep anyway, but for once I had important things to contemplate. When are we set to go?"

"As soon as I get the right equipment." Madame Wilson kissed Bastet on her nose. "I will be back soon."

"Oh – don't leave me alone please. I forgot to tell you about Claire."

But Madame Wilson was gone. And there was worse to come. She'd left her dratted dog, Necromancer, behind in the flat.

Bastet sat in the silence, anticipating the dog's move. Before too long, the door opened a sliver and Necromancer's muzzle appeared. She needed to stay calm. The dog was stupid; he only growled if she attracted attention to herself. She had to feign being a lifeless object.

"Bonjour, Madame Wilson!"

Oh no. It was that awful maid, Claire. How quietly she'd crept into the flat; the little sneak-thief.

"Ah-ha. I see my terrible boss has gone out again and left you all alone." Claire turned to Bastet with an insipid grin.

"Does that mean you have another nasty fate in store for me today?" said Bastet.

"Hmph. More than you can handle, you horrible little witch. I have a few tricks up my sleeve."

Bastet resigned herself to another day of merciless torment. She predicted Claire's next move and was right.

"Onto the carpet for you, you filthy vermin. And there you will stay while I clean."

Oh, if only she had the freedom of her four legs to escape. Bastet tried to hop off the sofa, but Claire caught her and threw her onto the floor in one powerful move. The horrible maid pulled a small glass bottle full of golden liquid out of her pocket. Was it perfume? Did Claire think she was smelly; perhaps want to sprinkle a Parisian fragrance onto her? Bastet watched her take off the lid. She closed her eyes as Claire emptied the contents over her face and body. An odorous whiff reached her nose. This was no perfume; it was urine.

"Necromancer, come here. Woo-ee, come here you silly dog!" Claire patted her legs, enticing the Westie over. "Did you know dogs are stupid? They only sense good or bad energy and they respond only to scent. That's why I got the pheromones of a large alpha-male Doberman. Now Necromancer will be forced to mark his territory."

Necromancer lowered his head, bared his teeth and growled at Bastet. Claire slapped him on his nose, forcing him into submission. She dragged him closer to Bastet by his collar. "Enough of that, you horrible mutt. Smell her."

Poor Necromancer. Even though she was afraid, Bastet couldn't help feeling sorry for him at his treatment. He sniffed, investigating her body, her head, her nose. Then he lifted his leg over her face.

"No, Necromancer, please no…"

Humiliation. Claire dropped to her knees, laughing. It was a terrible belly laugh making her rock on her haunches, making the punishment much worse, adding insult to injury. Bastet's bandages were soggy. She imagined the wetness in the corners of her eye sockets as tears flowing free.

Time for revenge. Bastet worked herself upright and sprang forward at Necromancer. Necromancer yelped and leaped at Claire. The dog was frenzied, ripping at her dress. She fell back screaming with him on top of her, biting her arm. Claire managed to rip him off with her other hand. She grabbed hold of his collar and flung him hard. Necromancer snarled and took charge again. Claire looked pale and shaken as she got to her feet and Bastet saw that her arm was bleeding badly. She flashed an evil look at Bastet before running out, with Necromancer fast at her heels.

***

Time seemed to follow its own schedule for the damned. The next couple of useless hours were a blink of an eye to a cat long dead the past three millennia. Bastet had lain, sodden, as Madame Wilson had come back. She'd listened to her mistress call out to her on finding the door open. Madame Wilson had listened as Bastet had relayed the story of how Necromancer had pursued Claire out the door. Bastet emphasised the details of Claire's treachery and felt satisfied that Madame Wilson would see the pitiless maid punished.

"Necromancer knows his way home. I am sure he gave her what she deserved. Nevertheless, I will see her punished for this myself. In the meantime, we have enough to contend with." Madame Wilson showed a chisel, a hammer and a trowel. "I took these from a friend's garage. I left him a note explaining their absence. He won't mind. Now let's go before the tourists impede our mission."

Madame Wilson tucked Bastet into her bag and made off for the catacombs. Not long now. Bastet didn't mind the swinging motion as her mistress walked, nor did the rumble and whine of the train bother her much. Her mind was on bigger things. She would soon be leaving the large, dreadful, modern city behind and heading for the tranquil, fertile valley of her sunny homeland.

"Bastet, my darling, Bastet. It's safe to come out now. We're here."

Madame Wilson opened her bag and revealed to Bastet a dark interior. There were disarticulated bones mounted in an array of gruesome shapes: circles, hearts, squares. The skulls of the unfortunate deceased lined the walls of the morbid display in unsavoury row upon row for the entertainment of the living. Bastet would have wrinkled her nose if it had not become an unobtrusive and emaciated article under her bandages. She didn't care much for the dead. She didn't care much to be dead either.

"Monsieur Dupree, where are you?" said Madame Wilson, in French.

"He's over here," said a husky male voice, also in English.

"Can you speak English, Monsieur Dupree? I have a visitor for you who doesn't know French well."

"Yes, I can speak English. I'm over here between the aviator and the cotton broker."

"And above the sculptor," added another voice. "Don't forget about me."

Bastet looked in the direction of the voices and saw a quartet of skulls in the converging V of a heart-shaped arrangement in the wall.

"Oh, how romantic," Madame Wilson cried.

"Indeed," said Bastet.

"How may I be of service?" asked Marcel Dupree.

"Well, how do I put this simply." Madame Wilson looked thoughtful. "We would like to rescue you from eternity in this crypt to take you on an Egyptian adventure."

"Fine by me. But may I ask why?" Marcel enquired.

"Here's the reason." Madame Wilson lifted Bastet from her bag. "I'd like to reunite her with her old mistress in Bubastis."

"Hello," said Bastet.

Marcel's jaw dropped until it dangled dangerously from its hinge.

"Extraordinary! I remember this cat. But I don't remember her speaking."

"I have always been linguistically adept." Bastet hesitated. "Though I haven't always been the most loquacious of speakers."

Madame Wilson smiled. "Good. Now that the pleasantries are over, Marcel, would you permit me to remove you from the wall?"

"I most certainly would, and I look forward to it too. It's not much fun being ogled by morbid tourists in this limbo, even with such fine company as I have had."

Madame Wilson took out her pick. "Just what I wanted to hear. Then let us begin."

***

Travelling was not as Bastet had expected. This time, not only was there no wooden crate, endless smoke and unfamiliar clatter of one monstrous transport carriage that Marcel Dupree kindly explained was a train, but there was no rocking motion nor smell of the sea. They weren't going by boat, Madame Wilson told her, they were going by plane.

Plane. A giant, noisy, silver bird of a thunderous beast. Bastet trembled in Madame Wilson's hand luggage. She wondered how poor Marcel was getting on in the cargo hold. Madame Wilson had had no choice but to check him in, she'd said, otherwise their trip would've been held up if she had had to explain having a skull in her baggage. Despite this, she had to pass him off as a fake tourist trinket to get him through check-in. And it was still better than poor Necromancer, left in the kennels for a month.

The plane touched down in Cairo. Bastet wondered if the excitement would explode out of her. Soon she would see the lush, green Nile valley, the pyramids, the sphinx. But as they descended from the silver bird, she was met with a vast, dirty city and beyond, miles and miles of endless desert.

Life had certainly changed.

Fear seized her for the first time. What if her mistress, the beautiful Nephthys, had been trapped forever under the foundation of some horrid modern building or buried under a relentless and unforgiving sand dune?

"Bastet, my love, what is it?" Madame Wilson asked.

Bastet couldn't control it. Her worries poured out.

"Yes, it's true. Only 10% of Ancient Egyptian tombs have been uncovered. But Bubastis was an important holy sanctuary. I severely doubt Nephthys would have been lost." Madame Wilson patted Bastet. "At any rate, we shall find out soon. I wish to call into the department of antiquities at Cairo Museum."

Bastet buried herself in the lining of Madame Wilson's bag. She'd come all this way, but now couldn't bear to face reality. She was sorry she hadn't remained buried in the temple all those years. If only she could hide from the world forever. Sooner or later, she knew she would have to emerge. It was only a matter of time before Madame Wilson lifted her out.

"I have a surprise for you."

She was inside a room filled with the dead; but this was no *Mastaba* full of mummies. The room was filled with strange modern machines. Bastet could only assume it was an examination room for antiquities. In front of them stood an open sarcophagus with a mummy inside. Her skin was hard and black and the hair was orange; most likely bleached through thousands of years of exposure to the elements.

"Oh, my gracious Bastet! My loving, beautiful, faithful companion," said the voice of Nephthys. Bastet looked at the mummy, but she didn't recognise her old mistress in the wizened speaker before her. The days of the beautiful, dark, kohl-lined eyes, deep brown skin and long, black hair were gone.

"Can it be you, my mistress?" said Bastet, in the old tongue. She found the words came back to her as she spoke, as though she'd never been away from Egypt.

"Yes, it is – oh my faithful companion, it's been too long."

Bastet wanted to weep, but her eyes remained dry. She wanted to curl up on Nephthys' lap, but remembered her legs were bound.

"Are you to be on display in the Cairo museum?" asked Bastet.

"I'm afraid so," said Nephthys.

Bastet looked around for help from Madame Wilson. Her new mistress came into the room a moment later with a broad smile on her face.

"What is it?" asked Bastet.

"I've just bought Nephthys for my private collection," said Madame Wilson.

"That's wonderful," Bastet cried. "But how…what–?"

Madame Wilson pulled a wad of cash from her wallet. "And that's not all. I won't be taking her back to France. I've decided to live here."

"How can you do that? You're not Egyptian." Bastet trailed off.

Behind Madame Wilson stood a man. He stepped out, making his appearance clear. The man and Madame Wilson smiled at each other. Bastet saw that they held hands.

"This is Mohamed. He is a curator here at Cairo Museum. He has invited us to stay with him. All of us – Nephthys, Marcel, and you too my love, my darling Bastet. If it wasn't for you wanting to come to Egypt,

I never would've met the man of my dreams. It was love at first sight."

***

The cruise ship sailed along the Nile. Mohamed and Madame Wilson clinked their champagne glasses. Marcel and Nephthys gazed across the water from where they were propped up against the rail of the deck. Bastet relaxed against her cushion and watched the two couples. They were all one big happy family.

"Nephthys," Madame Wilson started. "Bastet has one wish she would like fulfilled. Back in Paris, there was an evil woman who caused her much hurt and injustice. This same woman wronged my beloved dog, Necromancer. We would like to see her corrected for her evil actions."

"You wish me to place a curse on her?" asked Nephthys.

Madame Wilson lifted a roll of papyrus and a pen from her bag. "If you will dictate to me a suitable punishment, I will commit it to the gods."

"It will be done," said Nephthys, in the language of the ancients. "For the torment caused to my beautiful Bastet and the suffering inflicted upon you, I will cast upon her a curse of the destruction of Sekhemet, protector of the Pharoahs, lioness warrior goddess and healer of Bast. May she furthermore invoke the ire of Thoth who will seize her by the neck like a bird."

Madame Wilson wrote in hieroglyphs, guided by Mohamed's expertise. She cast the papyrus into the Nile. Bastet watched it float until it was consumed by the soft glow of the sunset. She'd never felt so content.

The moderns said cats had nine lives. If so, this was a good way to spend them.

The Barrow Bovidae

Dawn stood on the street corner, wearing her usual faded work jeans smeared with soil. Typical archaeologist's wardrobe. She looked up as I approached, tucked her plum-coloured fringe behind her ear and smiled.

"You're early for a change," I said.

"Did you remember all the stuff?"

I flipped my satchel open to show her the notepad, graph paper, measuring tape, pencil, eraser and torch.

"It's so good to be out of that stuffy office for a change," I said.

"I know, today's gorgeous," she said, smiling. "Where're we off to anyway?"

"Heading south. Apparently, there's some nice ones at the back of the graveyard."

My study of Mausoleums had taken me practically all over the county during June. Most of the tombs I had surveyed held the skeletons of couples who had owned considerable wealth during their lifetimes. How romantic. Or maybe ironic, considering I was now climbing inside the ancient coffins to take measurements with my ex-girlfriend in tow.

Dawn was a clingy sort of person. She had offered herself up as a volunteer to take notes for me, as I shouted out numbers in semi-darkness. Not too many girls would do such a task. Or maybe it was because of the perks to the job – like the fact that we had a casual thing going. My volunteer in more ways than one. In any case, she was happy with the arrangement, no strings attached and all that. Nothing a man could complain about, really.

The artistic study was coming along well. I would plot a scale version of the Mausoleum, then sketch in the intricate stonework of the façade later. I had covered a nice range of mausoleums in my study – from the more elaborate nineteenth century style crypts, to the simple, weatherworn tombs of the seventeenth century.

We went by bus. The journey took about forty minutes and was uneventful. We passed the house that I vowed I would one day own. I wondered how long it took to build it and what the perimeter measured. Dawn complained about her hay-fever. Once we got off, I navigated with my beat-up map and we found the forgotten graveyard down a stony lane.

My eyes scanned the scattered gravestones that were like small rain-worn hillocks dotted around the site.

"I don't see any Mausoleums here," I said, squinting against the afternoon light. "Do you?"

Dawn shook her head. "Looks like there could be a barrow up there, though." She pointed towards what looked like a miniature, grass-covered Ayers rock on top of the hill. It was partly hidden behind a clump of trees, but appeared to be no more than about fifteen feet long and about six feet high. The grassy hillock certainly did look like a long barrow. I jerked my bag up my shoulder and climbed the weed jungle of the hill with Dawn at my side.

As I approached, I noticed a metre-wide stone slab above two crudely hewn rectangular entrance posts, each no more than a half a metre thick. The passageway was blocked with soil and grass. Dawn and I worked to pull away the turf, until the entrance was clear.

"Weird," I said, scratching my ear. I bent down and entered through the narrow doorway. "Wonder why it isn't marked on the map?"

Dawn shrugged. "Might be an old map. They didn't bother with details on the older versions. No topography, nothing."

"Still, wouldn't they bother to put an obvious feature like this on a map? These little villages could do with the tourism."

"Maybe they didn't realise what it was. Could easily be an old bunker from the war, or a well-disguised public toilet."

"Probably been used as both of those at some point," I said, with a cautious sniff.

Dawn followed me inside. The light was dim, but I could make out what looked like two small chambers inside. Above, the low stone ceiling was covered with moss and the air reeked of earth. My foot crunched over rubble on the ground. Looking down, I could make out disarticulated bones.

Dawn bent down and picked up a fragment. She turned the piece over in her hand, observing it with wide eyes in the poor light. "It's got cut marks on it. Probably de-fleshed."

I nodded, noting the array of large and small scattered remains. "Adult and child."

"There's another chamber across there, did you see?" she asked.

Still ducking, we entered the second small enclosure. More scattered bones. Some appeared to have been burnt.

"It seems odd that all this is just lying here so open and none of it has been recorded," I said, more careful than I had been in the first chamber to step around the bones.

I spun around looking for Dawn and couldn't see her. The line of light from the almost obscured doorway now provided an eerie glow inside the barrow.

"Did you know that in ancient times people used to think chambered tombs were supernatural, otherworldly places?" Dawn's voice had a ghostly resonance as it reached me from the other chamber.

"Aren't they?" I said, touching the walls of the tomb. "They're burial places, after all."

"I meant evil," she said. "You know that poem 'Sir Gawain and the Green Knight'? Well, the Knight supposedly lived in, how does it go, a 'rounded mound on the side of a slope that was overgrown with grass and quite hollow inside'. And apparently there was a long barrow in Beowulf too. Some sort of Dragon lived in it. That was its lair."

Her voice seemed amplified in the narrow space and assaulted my ears. I winced as the onset of a headache swept over me. My hand reached for my forehead in the gloom and felt it to be clammy.

"Gareth, get back here, I think there's something else."

My feet led me out of the right anterior chamber and shuffled across the uneven ground as if they were detached from my body, much like the assortment of bones all around me. I could make out Dawn's form at the back of the enclosure. My eyeballs shook for a moment as I struggled to focus on her in the gloom. I rubbed them with my thumb and forefinger, blinked long and hard and walked towards her.

Squiggles. Zigzagging shapes danced before my eyes on the walls of the tomb, delving into the shadows of the crypt. "Dawn, I need fresh air."

"I think it's a Cist, Gareth. There's a skeleton, mostly intact, no hands and feet though."

"I feel a bit sick-"

"Shut up, just a bit longer. What do you reckon this is? There's something on the skull."

I felt her hand in the semi-darkness guide mine towards the skull which was set in a shallow pit. Two small objects were lodged up the nasal cavity of the skull.

Swirling shapes, like snail shells flittered before my heavy-lidded eyes. "I dunno, maybe finger bones. They probably shoved the person's hands in their nose to prop the head up." My own head rolled on my shoulders. "Can we go? I think I have altitude sickness."

I could sense Dawn's face turned towards me in the dark. "Altitude sickness? It's only a small hill. What's wrong with you? Are you scared of ghosts or what?"

I heard the rustle of her clothes as she turned back towards the skull. "You're right, I think. They're small bones, very fragmented. Phalanges, but I don't think they're human. I wish there was more light in here. Gimme your torch."

I fumbled in my satchel and closed my fingers around the plastic handle. My hand shook as I lifted it out and it slipped out of my grip. The clatter of the torch rolling across the floor was a firecracker going off in my ears.

"Oh Gareth, you lost it," Dawn whined. I heard her sigh. "Never mind. This is really exciting."

She hummed as she examined the bones. "There's part of a jaw in this pit. I think it's a sheep. But why was the person buried with a sheep? More to the point, why did they have the sheep's toes shoved up their nose?"

Which way was out? Which direction was I pointing in? We were in the posterior chamber, there was a Cist. I needed to steady myself.

I stretched my arms wide, but felt no walls. I reached up and felt the rough stone ceiling, strewn with hard protrusions. The objects were wide at the base, tapering off towards the end. I knew they weren't stone, but wasn't sure what they were. They felt like the dried pig's ears my parents' dog liked to chew.

"What's this?" said Dawn's voice. It seemed she had found the strange stalactites. I heard a crunching sound in the hollow space. "Tastes like, I don't know what. Fat."

"Fat?" I grabbed her arm, my fingers feeling along it towards her mouth. "What the hell are you eating them for? They could be anything! Parts of human corpses, for all we know."

"Ooh, evaporated fat. Maybe they cremated the body in here and the solids floated up and formed this lovely layer."

My heavy breath clouded the air around me with diamond-shaped patterns. Was I hearing her right? "Dawn, we need to get outside. I think I'm not in my right mind."

"Or maybe both were buried together," she said, "because both died together." Another crunch.

I realised my fingers were still linked around her wrist, the tips of each cold. I yanked on Dawn's arm and led her towards the light.

"We need to get more stuff and come back to survey this place properly," she said. "Mmm, you should try these. They're really tasty."

The crisp sound of munching met my ears. I shook her by the wrist and she let go of her grisly snack, sending the morsel flying.

"Those stories are right – this place is making us mad!" I said, leading her outside.

As I came outside and straightened up to my full height, I noticed that my hand, still holding onto Dawn behind me, was dragging me down. I looked back. I was no longer holding onto Dawn, but rather, a small brown hairy sheep, standing on its rear legs because of my grip on its hoof. Its long legs and shaggy coat gave it a somewhat wild appearance and as it looked up at me, it tipped its curly head.

"Dawn!" I said, letting go with a jolt. "What the-?!"

"Ga-a-a-reth," she said, in a bleating voice. "It's that food I ate. It was fu-u-u-nny."

I ran both hands through my hair and stared at the animal. "What happened to you – you're a primitive sheep!"

"I don't know what happened."

Magic. It had to be. Druid magic, or whatever else. Those geometric shapes I'd seen. The tales of supernatural events.

"Did you eat one of the sheep bones?"

"No-o-o," she said in a quaver. "Only the stuff on the ceiling."

"But you must've said something. I dunno, think. An incantation. Something to seal the spell."

"Last thing I said was 'both died together' about the human and sheep bones."

"Both died together, both died..." I said, thinking. "That's it! I've got it! Bovidae! That must be it! You said the magic words while eating part of the human-sheep conglomeration."

"So now what?"

I shrugged. "Guess you're stuck as a sheep."

Dawn always did follow me around as one, so this would be no different. Sort of.

"Well, at the very least, could we find out what kind of sheep I am?"

I nodded. "We have the harder job first, of getting you home."

My fears were confirmed. The bus driver wouldn't let me take Dawn onboard, even when I put my sunglasses on and pretended she was my guide-sheep. We managed to hitch a ride in the back of a truck for part of the way, and then walked the rest.

"Don't drop turds on the footpath," I said. "You'll embarrass me. If you need to go, find a bush."

Dawn responded with an assortment of pebble-sized black balls of different sizes.

"I couldn't help it," she said, with a cry. "This body is hard to control. I haven't got the hang of it yet."

I walked on, letting her trail behind. "Well, if you do it in my flat, you can clean it yourself."

Once we got to my place, I dumped my bag by the front door and grabbed one of the reference books off my shelf. Leafing through the section on animal domestication, I found what I suspected.

"You're a mouflon. The ancestor of the domestic sheep," I said, snapping the book closed.

Dawn looked up at me, sheepishly. "Oh well. Can I stay with you until we figure this all out?"

I rolled my eyes. "You practically live here anyway," I said. "Only you can't stay in my bed anymore. I'm many things, but not a sheep-shagger. And you'll need to pay your way. Do you provide milk or something?"

The sheep let its mouth fall open, showing a fine diastema. "The cheek! Animal husbandry and you aren't even my husband. Fine! Then you certainly can't milk me!" She stomped out of the room. "I'm going to use the toilet!"

"Well, do it in the bowl, not on the floor."

"I am house-trained, you know! This body might be awkward and clumsy for me but my memory's still intact."

I put my head in my hands. What was I going to do?

Then I remembered – Uncle Roger. He was a sheep farmer in Bury St. Bellwether. He would know what to do. Maybe not how to change her back to human form, but at least how to manage her.

"I'm going out to see someone," I yelled towards the bathroom. "I'll be back in a while. Don't put hoof prints all over the pâté while I'm gone!"

I swung the door shut behind me to a chorus of protests from Dawn. Dawn the human liked pâté – but would she still like it as a sheep? Sheep were herbivores of course, but then, Dawn wasn't a normal one. What did sheep even eat? Uncle Roger would sort it all out for me.

The walk to his farm took a good half an hour along tree lined lanes and gravelly paths that turned among the hedgerows. The farmhouse was set close to the road. I pushed the huge metal gate open and let it fall closed behind me. Then I approached the front door and knocked.

"Aunt Patty," I said, panting from my walk. "Is Uncle Roger busy?"

"No, come on in, love," she said, kissing my cheek. She turned, looking up the stairs. "The lad's here to see you!"

"The lad?"

"Gareth!" She said, then turned back to me. "He'll be down in a minute. You come on through."

I sat down in their cosy sitting room. Now that I was there, what would I say? I couldn't admit that my ex-lover was a mouflon or it would raise all sorts of ugly questions. Better to start with the basics.

"Uh, hello Uncle."

Uncle Roger sat down, filling most of the chair with his bulk. "Gaz, it's good to see ya. Still doing that course at college?"

"Eh, yeah, nearly finished. Actually, I came here to ask you something about sheep."

Uncle Roger laughed, phlegm rattling around in his chest. "Sheep? I doubt that's for your course, is it?"

"Well, kind of. No, it isn't. Just curiosity. I'm minding a pet sheep for a friend and wondered how to take care of it, that's all."

Uncle Roger stood up as quickly as he had sat down. "Are you staying for dinner then? This could take a while."

I rubbed my hands together, thinking of Dawn back in my flat. "Uh, yeah. Yeah, why not."

"Well, your visits are so few and far between, I'd better cook up a feast. You catch up with your aunt there and I won't be two shakes of a lamb's tail."

Aunt Patty and I got caught up over several cups of tea while Uncle Roger busied himself out back. "He's probably getting one fresh for you," she said.

"Didn't know he slaughtered them too?"

"He does most stuff himself," she said, grinning.

Soon, the delicious smell of cooking lamb enticed us into the kitchen. I could see in the pan, three good-sized steaks sizzling away.

"Look's a treat," I said, my mouth watering. "I can't wait to tuck in."

Aunt Patty and I helped set the table and we ate a proper meal in the dining room. The meat was fresh and tender and nicely herbed.

"You'll have to show me how to cook lamb," I said. "Your sheep really are the best quality."

Uncle Roger shoved a fork-load into his mouth. "Oh this one wasn't mine. I ran her over when I was going up the hill to get one of my lot to cook for your tea. She wasn't marked, but I can't be sure she wasn't from one of the neighbouring farms, so I thought I'd get rid of the carcass, you know how it goes with fresh road-kill." He winked. "Must've got in through the front gate. You left it open on your way in. Sometimes I think you were born in a barn, lad!"

I swallowed my food as Uncle Roger laughed, and felt my stomach sink with the weight of his words.

"Was she a small ewe, kind of brownish with long legs?" I said, in a choked voice.

"That's right. Did you see it?"

My throat felt tight. My mouth opened wide and I clutched my neck with both hands as I tried to dislodge the chunk of Dawn that sat behind my tonsils. I saw Aunt Patty reach across the table and Uncle Roger race around the edge towards me. The room was closing in. Spirals, diamonds and pyramids of hardened tissue hung like stalactites before my eyes. Zigzagging shapes danced before my eyes, leading me towards the barrow. And behind the barrow at the top of the hill, a thin line of light welcomed me towards it.

The Woman and the Stiff

"What a salubrious day."

"I said, what a salubrious day. Would you care to vum me a cigarette?"

In the egg-yolk glow of sunset, a man stood admiring his stark silhouette. Even though it was drawn out by the evening, it still looked a hell of a lot beefier than his meagre frame. The woman in front of him looked up with a frown as his shadow passed over her.

"You mean 'bum'," she said.

He sat down next to her on the metal bench. "Usually I don't talk to strangers," he said, "But I must say, I've had a life altering experience and I see things a lot differently now."

She gave him a cigarette and offered a light, hoping he wouldn't try to continue the conversation. Her book was getting to an interesting part. But as the tip of his cigarette began to glow, she found her head turning. Able to resist it no longer, her eyes travelled up the length of the rolled tobacco towards his mouth. His lips were shrivelled, curled back from his teeth. Brown decayed gums were exposed, and a row of rotting logs that would give a dentist a field day.

"Bad lip balm," said the guy before a hiss broke from his throat, giving way to rattling rasps.

The woman cocked her head, raising one eyebrow. She found his appearance somewhat strange. A pair of oversized aviators covered most of his face, perched above a rather non-existent nose. What was with the sunglasses? It was twilight already.

"Who are you?"

As he turned his head and looked her full in the face, she heard the soft groan of stretching leather. But his trench coat was made of cotton. Wasn't it?

"Are you from Germany?" she asked. Their eyes met. At least, she thought they did. Hard to tell behind his thick black shades.

"What made you assume that?"

"Your accent. You said 'vum' instead of bum."

"That must be because of my hare lip."

That's some hare lip, she thought.

An ardent breeze stirred, inspiring leaves to dance around their feet. The woman was caught downwind of her strange companion's cigarette smoke and a scent she couldn't quite fathom. Musty. Like compost. But tinged with something else. There was definitely an aftertaste. Bitter.

"Who *are* you?" she asked.

"I'm Alfred." His grin was mottled umber; a perfect poster of tooth decay. Compelled by an invisible force, she snatched off his glasses.

Sockets. Lined with shrivelled lids, flaccid skin. Sunken dehydrated eyes, clouded like cataracts.

"You're dead!"

"No need to get personal."

She grappled with the bench, a flurry of metal and hands, trying to put as much distance between herself and the corpse. Yet running wasn't an option. Scared; yes, she couldn't deny it, but she had to know more about him. Morbid curiosity overruled fear.

"How can this be? This isn't possible."

"Well *obviously* you need to check again love, because here I am."

"Don't look at me like that; it gives me the creeps."

The stiff swelled with indignation. "Couldn't you be more sympathetic? I went through a lot before I came to be in my present condition."

"How did you – well, how did you come to be like this? A talking corpse, I mean?"

He puffed up again and snapped his sunglasses back on. "It wasn't easy, I'll say that."

"How long've you been, y'know, dead?"

He shrugged, unleashing a fresh whiff of putrid flesh.

"A long time. I don't keep a diary in the afterlife." He chuckled and started coughing violently. "If you have time, I'll tell you the strangest tale you'll ever hear. I can guarantee you that."

"I'm listening," she said, closing her book.

"Well, a while back – actually, a good while back – I was out having a nice drive with the missus. Wanna see a picture of me back then?" He reached into his pocket and rummaged about. "Damn it, where's that bloody thing got to?"

The woman stared, transfixed in horror as he opened his jacket revealing a gaping hole with yellowed skin, peeled back like a month-old tomato. The remnants of a tattered shirt hung like a morbid curtain, partly obscuring the grisly sight.

"That was when my stomach exploded. Bodies, eh? Why do they accumulate all the mush and juice and gases if they can't handle the shit that comes with it? Anyway, where was I?"

"You were going to show me your photo."

"Ah, here it is." He reached into the hole and retrieved his wallet. The woman felt like she was staring into a cesspit.

"Tricky little sucker," he said, laughing. "Gets lost in all manner of nooks and crannies."

Trying desperately not to think of what kinds of orifices a corpse possessed, she took his old driving license from him.

"See any resemblance?" he chuckled.

The picture was faded, long since exposed to the ravages of river water and rotten kidneys. The face was barely discernible, but what she could make out looked like a moderately attractive man of around thirty-two or thirty-three years of age with dark hair and blue eyes.

"Not bad," she said, handing it back. The corpse grimaced. She took his expression as one of pleasure.

"Yes, I was a looker back then. Too bad we can't keep our charms, eh?"

The woman gave a weak smile. Understatement of the year, in her opinion.

"So anyway, since it was getting late, we decided to head back home. We were crossing a bridge when I noticed a group of teenage boys hanging about. One of them had a rock in his hand. Can you believe the little bastard lobbed it at my car?"

"So what did you do?"

"A lot of bloody damage to my tyres as I screeched to a halt, I can tell you that! I got out and chased the boy and... well, here I am."

"What, that's it? That doesn't explain anything. How'd you get killed? I assume you were murdered?"

The corpse sighed, air rattling out of his ossified windpipe. "Yes, of course I was murdered. After I stopped the car, I tore off after the kids."

"You already explained all this-"

"I'm getting to it!" snapped the corpse with a puff of powdered cilia. "As I was saying, I caught up with the gang and grabbed the boy by the scruff of his neck. But the others, they attacked me with sticks and rocks. And then I saw a concrete slab aimed at my head, coming towards my face. After that, there was blackness."

The woman sat, grim faced.

"I suppose that's when I died," he said sadly.

"Did you feel your soul leaving your body?"

"Actually no, I didn't. I just sort of opened my eyes. And when I came to, I saw water rushing towards me.

Black water. Torrents of it. It was then that I realised I'd been tipped off the bridge."

The woman clapped her hand to her mouth. "How awful!"

"Do you wanna know the funny thing about being the living dead?" he asked. "It's that you wake up, if you call it waking up of course, and realise you can't feel a thing. No senses. No pain. I couldn't even taste the blood gushing from the open wound on my hairline."

He lifted back his hair and the woman rested her eyes upon the San Andreas fault of all wounds. She assumed the solidified black lump was long ago congealed blood.

"So why did you ask for a cigarette then?"

"Habit. I suppose. It's not like I'm gonna die of lung cancer, eh?" He wheezed, his body racked with laughter. The woman didn't find it in the least bit funny.

"I floated for eons you know. Night and day became one massive fucking hell."

A small white fleck crawled out of his left nostril. At first the woman thought it was snot. Since when did corpses have snot? But then she saw him flick it off his face and realised it was a maggot. She flinched. Just missed her cheek.

"You'd think they would find me, but they didn't. By the time I regained the use of my legs, it was too late to go wandering back into my wife's life. Can you imagine it? 'Honey, I'm home'!"

"Yeah, I don't think that would've gone down well," she agreed.

"So instead, I sat by the river among the bulrushes rethinking my death. I suppose all that time spent in the sun and silt kind of mummified me. At least that's my theory to explain the emaciation. And look at my hair, bleached by the elements. Best highlights you could ever ask for. Women would kill to have these locks and it didn't cost me a thing."

"So why are you back?" she asked. "I've heard that ghosts have to walk the earth until they finish what they came here to do or something like that. Is it the same with corpses?"

"I guess so."

The woman was silent, thinking. "I get it. You've come back to take revenge on the ones who killed you."

The stiff shuddered. "Now that's just creepy!" He shifted in his seat and composed himself again. "Initially it did cross my mind. But I did a lot of thinking and decided that if they killed me once when I was strong and fit, what would they do to me now? No, I'm back for a greater purpose."

"What's that?"

"I'm back to educate people on the dangers of road rage." And with that, he made his way along the riverside path towards the main road into town.

The Lady and the Tiger

The glass tower block, called The City, shone before me in the morning sun. I popped a mint into my mouth and took a deep breath, then climbed the front steps and walked through the revolving doors into a wide lobby. My interview letter said I had to go to the thirtieth floor, so I made my way to the lifts to the left of the reception desk.

I pushed the button and waited. The doors opened and I saw a smartly-dressed woman in her mid-thirties, wearing a tweed jacket and pinstripe trousers. Next to her, on a leash, was a Siberian tiger.

"Are you getting in?" she asked me.

"Really? Is it safe?" I replied.

She smiled. "Sure. A lady can't be a lady without her tiger. And a tiger needs a lady for balance. Up or down?"

"But- aren't we on the ground floor?"

She shook her head. "No, it gets much lower than this. Rock bottom."

I wasn't sure what she meant, but I got in and stood with the tiger to my right. I raised my hand towards the panel on the left side, but noticed that the numbers only went as high as twenty-five. The doors closed, but the lift didn't move.

"How do I get to the thirtieth floor?" I asked her.

"You take the lift," she said.

I frowned. "It doesn't go up there."

"Up where?"

"To the thirtieth floor."

"What about it?"

I paused, not sure if she was playing a game with me. "I need to get to the thirtieth floor."

"Do you?" she said, smiling.

I could feel my blood rising; in a new place, with no help, being toyed with by a lady and her tiger.

"Can you tell me how to get to the thirtieth floor?" I snapped.

"You take the lift," she said.

I pushed the button to open the door and shook my head as I walked out. On the right side of the reception desk, I spotted a door that I had not seen from the entrance. A tall, handsome black man opened the door and came out.

"You must be Cora?" he said.

"Yes, I'm here for an interview. But it was supposed to be on the thirtieth floor."

"Not yet," he said smiling. "Ms. Leading will see you first."

He pushed the door wide, letting me enter a small room lit by a phosphorescent tube above. There was no furniture in the small, silvery space. A large poster with the word 'pre-contemplation' hung on the wall opposite the door. A bowl of round, white sweets sat on the floor below it.

"What does that poster mean?" I asked.

"You're on the right side now," said the man. "What do you think?"

Right side? Of the reception desk? "Er- pre-contemplation means denial, doesn't it?"

"Right," he answered. "Ms. Leading is waiting for you. Help yourself to a sweet while you're waiting."

He closed the door and I saw a full length mirror on the back of it. Ms. Leading was nowhere to be seen. I took a sweet from the bowl and swallowed it; chalky, and surprisingly bland under the sugary coating. Instinct brought me towards the mirror. My reflection looked back at me.

"Hello," said my face in the mirror. "You must be Cora."

"What's going on? Am I dreaming?"

"No, I thought you knew; Pre-contemplation. You're working."

"I am? On what?"

My reflection smiled back. "Through some stuff. I'm Ms. Leading."

She extended her hands towards me; I watched her fingers pierce the membrane of the mirror, and jumped as they stretched into my world.

"Don't be alarmed. I'm here to help you."

"What do you mean, I'm working? If this isn't a dream, then what… am I knocked out?"

She smiled. "No. You came here for an interview. I'll show you what to do next."

"How do I know I can trust you?"

"Do you trust yourself?" she said.

I shrugged. She still hadn't answered my question. Was I daydreaming?

Ms. Leading pulled herself out of the mirror and stood face to face with me. I stood rooted to the spot as she moved closer. My skin tingled cold as she stepped into me; I found myself unable to speak.

I staggered a few steps and looked down at my body. Ms. Leading had filled a gap in me, giving me a better perspective on myself, helping my self-exploration.

I walked out of the room back into the lobby. The handsome man who had shown me to Ms. Leading stood behind the reception desk, smiling.

"Ms. Understanding is waiting for you. Best take some more sweets with you," he said, giving me a handful of the white, sugary balls. "You know where to go, I assume?"

Did I? My feet seemed to think so, as they led me towards the lift. "I'm not dreaming and I'm not dead," I said. "But since I don't know what's going on, I'll go with my feelings on this," I said. The man nodded and gestured towards the lift.

It was empty. I swallowed another sweet and pushed the button for floor twenty-five.

Twenty-three. Twenty-four. Twenty-five. When the doors opened, I found myself in a short corridor. A conference room stood through a door to the left. Looking through the small window in the door, I saw a long table. Thirty people sat around it; men and women, black and white. At the far side of the room stood the lady who I had met in the lift, writing a poem on a flipchart. The Siberian tiger sat next to the flipchart, intently watching the viewers. The lady began reciting the poem.

... The best way to go through life,
is like butter on a knife...

The words were muffled. I pushed the door open to hear more clearly.

... It coats the edge, although serrated
and smoothes the path, despite what's fated...

I stepped into the room.

"But that doesn't make sense," I said. "If the knife cuts the butter, how can the butter coat the knife?"

The viewers turned to me and the tiger let out a low growl, but the lady smiled.

"The butter melts and flows into the grooves," she said. "It is adaptable, unlike the hard steel knife."

"I'd rather be hard to face life than something that has to adhere to the shape of other things."

She shook her head. "You don't understand. You keep going left, but what you need is to balance it with right. You aren't ready."

"Ready for what?"

"The thirtieth floor. You should go. Your lift is waiting."

I looked at the faces around the table and my eyes stopped on details. One of the women near the door had a small, heart-shaped face and a heavy fringe. Through the parting in her fringe I could see another face, half-hidden on her forehead. If she tilted her head back, the features became clearer, dominating the face below. Two of the men sitting at the table were police officers. They stood up, seized me by my arms and dragged me from the room. I was powerless to resist.

"Hey, I don't want to go," I said, as they forced me down the corridor towards the lift. "You have no right to do this. I came here to see Ms. Understanding. Where's Ms. Understanding?"

The officers shoved me into the lift. I banged the back of my head against the wall and winced as the shiny doors slid shut and the lift descended. I hadn't pushed any buttons and neither had the officers, but I knew where I was going. Rock bottom.

The lift stopped and the doors opened. I could make out a dark, stone basement; the light from the lift didn't reach the corners of the room. I shuffled into the gloom with my arms outstretched.

"Hello? Is anyone there? Ms. Understanding?" I said.

"Look to the left," said my voice. My voice? I hadn't spoken.

"No, right first," I said again. The voice of my unconscious?

"Left, right, which one first?" I asked. "What's the difference?"

"Left brain, right brain. You're operating under the logical centre at the moment, Lefty. But you need to enter the creative hemisphere. So take another sweet and come this way," said the first speaker and it dawned on me at last; I was talking to myself.

"Wait a minute… these aren't sweets. What are they?"

"Just a little something to help you on your trip. What are you hiding from us?"

"Us? Who else is here? There's two of you, I thought—"

In the faint light from the open lift, six of me appeared in different colours: black, brown, gold, red, yellow and white. They encircled me, closing in.

"See the bigger picture: step outside yourself," said White and stepped into me.

"This is the way things are," said Yellow as we merged.

"Keep it all in focus," said Red and blended into me.

"Emotional states are no more mystical than physical states," said Gold and shimmered around me.

"There is something to learn from all things, however menial," said Brown as we connected.

"Take a trip through your mind," said Black and engulfed me.

I was alone. At my feet, I found an effigy of myself; a doll. The porcelain looked as real as my skin and the hair was exactly like mine. As I stooped to pick it up, words escaped my mouth.

The doll's name materialised in my mind. "Ms. Understanding."

I returned to the brightness of the lift with the doll in my hand. There was no number thirty on the panel and there never would be. Instead, I pushed the button for the ground floor. When the lift stopped, I walked across the lobby.

On the way out, I noticed the tall black man standing by the revolving doors. He smiled as I passed him into broad sunlight.

"Well done," he said, "You've figured out how the compartments work."

"I know I have to reach my destination another way. I accept that," I said.

"Good. She's waiting for you."

I walked around the right side of the glass tower block. Scaffolding stretched to the top of the building. A rope ladder hung from the topmost trestle.

I looked at the round, white sweets in my left hand. Taking one would have given me the courage I needed for the climb. But on the other hand–

I let them scatter on the ground and stepped on them, crushing them into a fine powder. I didn't need any help. I could do it by myself. I had my doll, Ms. Understanding, wedged under my right armpit.

I climbed onto the rope ladder and pushed upwards with my heels on each rope-step. The climb was slow; the wind blew and the sun glared. Along the way, I passed the outlines of dozens of people in their offices inside the tower block, busying about their lives, oblivious to all that happened outside.

I reached the window of the topmost floor. Inside, I recognised seven of the thirty people from the conference room on the twenty-fifth floor. They were all seated, and the woman from the lift lectured them from a podium near the door. There was no sign of her tiger.

She spotted me and opened the window. I took her hand as I climbed inside and walked to towards her on the far side, holding Ms. Understanding in my right hand.

"You've made it. Welcome to the thirtieth floor."

"Thank you," I said. I sighed with relief. "Have I missed any of your teachings?"

"Not yet, you're in time."

"Wait a minute, where's your tiger? You told me when we met that a lady needed her tiger for balance."

Her gaze rested on a point behind me, beneath the small window I had crawled through. The hairs on the back of my neck rose under a wave of hot breath. I shuddered. I knew it had been lurking in a shadowy corner. I knew it had been waiting for me. I turned. The huge, striped animal padded towards me. The shock of the dustbin-sized head coming towards me made me hold Ms. Understanding in front of me, for protection. Tucked in a pocket on the doll's dress was a single sweet. I popped it in my mouth and turned away curling into a ball, hoping the sweet would magic the tiger away. From the corner of my eye, I saw its strong jaws open wide. I felt the sharp teeth pierce the back of my neck. As the tiger crushed my spine, I crushed the sweet in my mouth and held Ms. Understanding in my left hand. Blackness swirled. And then I fell.

Death to an Idol

I worry. I worry a lot. I worry that my story will have no direction. I worry that the story I'm about to tell you doesn't make any sense. I'm too pedantic. But not too pedantic to stop telling my story. No, never that pedantic.

The moon was high in the sky. It hung behind a thin veil of fog. Not fog; fog is on the ground. This was cloud. It hung behind a thin veil of cloud.

I looked at the moon and I wanted to reach it. I stretched my fingers towards it and it slipped between my index and ring finger. It fit snugly in the V. Snugly.

Smugly. Snugly because it sat comfortably on the web of skin. Smugly because the moon mocked me. It mocked me like the prostitute who was ten pounds too dear for my miserly budget.

I did it. I did it again. I've made myself worry. I was getting into the groove of my story and I worked myself up all over again. I told you too much. I told you about the prozzie who was out of reach.

She was out of reach and she mocked me, like the moon. Her teeth were white, like the moon. And the bruise on her thigh was yellow; piss-coloured. A faded, piss-coloured stain as yellow as my cat's eyes.

My cat will probably eat me when I'm gone. Cats eat meat, and when I go, I will be meat. There's no reason that I can surmise as to why my cat would not eat my decaying remains after I'm gone.

Now I've done it. I've put you off. I don't know you, but I can tell I've made you want to stop reading my story. Or maybe I've got you wrong; you know my true nature now, but still you want to keep reading. You know I'm weird, so you're willing to see where this is all going.

Alright. So here it goes.

I read a story once about a girl who took the moon out of the sky and had it mounted on a necklace - or so she thought. I'd never want to keep the moon all to myself. I'm not the type of person who would think of myself as selfish like that. But am I as selfish as that? I suppose if I'm thinking about it, I must be.

I looked at the sky and realised the moon had gone. Venus was in its place. Or maybe the moon had never really been there in the first place. Nothing in my life was as it seemed anyway. I hired the whore because I was worried that I was a thirty year old virgin. I'm a virgin and a loser with women and I had to know what it felt like to fuck a woman. But, like the moon she had gone. In place of her, I found a white stairway.

The white stepping-stones led to Venus. On either side of the chalky discs, lava flowed, dark and thick. The waterfall flowed straight from the mouth of Vulcan. I worried that I might not reach the top in time and the flow would stop. The stepping-stones were beginning to sizzle as the lava burned at them.

I reached the top of the stairs – a hundred and twenty in total – and found a fountain. I scooped handfuls of the dark, red liquid into my mouth; it wasn't lava, it was wine. The wine poured out of the fountain and washed down the stairs, dissolving each disc-shaped step. It was too late now; I'd gone too far. I'd have to go all the way.

A forest lay ahead, a forest of women and money. The tree-trunks were their curvaceous bodies, the branches their slender arms. Their fingers dangled ten-pound notes as leaves, but every leaf was beyond my grasp. I didn't care anyway. Where I was going, these things were no good.

I looked down. My feet crunched over small pieces of broken glass. Broken bottles? But then I remembered; I was on my way to Venus, a volcanic planet. They had to be pieces of irregular-shaped, brown crystal that could have been smashed shards from an empty bottle of wine, or two.

As I picked one up, I cut my wrist on the surrounding pieces. Three parallel lines ran along the length of my wrist to the middle of my forearm.

My blood flowed freely, like the wine from the fountain. I splashed some upwards, staining the money-leaves held by the women. I was pleased to see that in my own way, I had reached the dozens of notes, even if I couldn't have them.

Yet again, I worried. Why were the cuts on my wrist so precise? So clinical. If it had been an accidental cut on the irregular-shaped crystals, the incisions would have been random, not deliberate.

I staggered on, dripping blood. I had to reach Venus, I absolutely had to. The money-forest was gone now and all I could see was a bottle, sitting on a rock table.

The bottle contained a strong-smelling, dark green liquid, a hint of pine meeting my nose. Maybe the contents would disinfect my cuts. I worried about my cuts. But by this stage in my journey, I couldn't say why.

I poured the glutinous liquid onto my wrist. I felt the sting in my wounds and winced.

I set the bottle down and when I stood up, I found that I was growing. I was towering, a giant, like Ajax in the Iliad. I was Ajax, from the bottle. The blood in my veins ran black.

I was no longer worried. The worry had gone away. I was invincible. Ajax ran in my veins. Soon it would erupt out of me and I realised I wasn't going to find Vulcan on Venus. I *was* Vulcan. I was the volcano, full of powerful liquid, ready to erupt. Out of me would spew forth a river of ecstasy. A pyroclastic flow that would run all over the heavenly body.

The ground was shaking, trembling, and I felt myself grow hot. Hot and sleepy. My eyes were blurring in and out of focus. Not yet. Not yet. The eruption hadn't come. It needed to come first. I needed to come.

Release. Warm, sticky white liquid splattered me. What was this? Not lava, but I knew what it was. The thought gave me pleasure and shame.

I stood huge over the landscape and saw Venus lie before me: glorious and blue. Across the barren landscape prowled a single cat. A tabby cat. My cat.

The worry was back, but this time mingled with a pleasant sleepiness that was slowly consuming me. The cat was trapped. Without me, it couldn't escape Venus. It had no food. No food until I was gone. Then I would become its food.

Sleepiness swirled. I sank to my knees, slumped onto my side, then lay flat on my back, letting my arms and legs fall loose. None of it mattered anymore – it was done. There were no stairs left; they had dissolved. There was no wine left; I had drunk it. There was no Ajax left; it was in me. Soon, nothing would remain of me either, for the cat would eat me.

Venus. I was on Venus, blue and ethereal. I was on Venus, the most beautiful and perfect of all the heavenly bodies. She didn't reject me. I idolised her and I knew for a fact that my love would be reciprocated. I wasn't worried, but it wouldn't have mattered anyway. It didn't matter where I was going.

Zombie Reflux

Eric sat in the waiting room of A&E, clutching his stomach. What in the hell was wrong with him?

"Mr. Von Pfeffer?" called the nurse. "The doctor will see you now."

Eric followed her into a room and sat on the doctor's bed. He caught sight of his reflection in the mirror. Sallow.

"Hello, you must be Mr. Von Pfeffer? How are you feeling?"

"Not good. It's my belly. I've had a lot of stomach problems lately."

The doctor produced a stethoscope. "I'm just going to listen to your abdomen, if you'll take off your shoes and lie down. It could be gastritis. Have you been having acid reflux?"

"Not that I was aware of." Eric slipped off his sandals and stretched out. The doctor placed the metal disc on his belly. He didn't even feel the coldness he had expected. His body was numb, detached.

The doctor paled. He lifted the stethoscope away.

"We have a problem, Mr. Von Pfeffer," said the doctor hurriedly. He looked across at paperwork on his desk and whispered to the nurse, who lingered near the door. She looked at Eric, and he could see confusion on her face.

"What is it, doctor?" said Eric.

"Er... I'm not sure. It could be my stethoscope is broken."

"Just tell it to me straight, please."

"Alright then. You have no heartbeat."

Eric stared at him. "What?"

The nurse pointed to his exposed stomach. Her words came out too hushed to hear. And then she fainted. The doctor's head turned a fraction towards her, but Eric noticed he couldn't take his eyes off him.

Eric's eyes travelled down his own body. A piece of brown leather rope was stuck to his midriff. He grasped it and pulled. It stretched, but didn't detach from his stomach.

And then he saw a hairline fracture, running across his midriff. Eric's jaw fell open. The object wasn't a leathery rope. It was his intestines poking out of his torso, like freeze-dried tripe.

"Oh God, oh my God! But, but how? It's not possible!"

The doctor stood, eyes fixed on Eric's protruding intestines. "You're a walking miracle. This must be a new kind of super-immunity, perhaps to an illness – perhaps even to–"

Eric flapped his hands. "Well, do something about it. Fix me! At the very least put my bowels back in, please!"

"I can't. Not until we run some tests," said the doctor, matter-of-factly.

Guinea pig. Eric jumped up, dislodging a tray of nasty-looking utensils from a medical trolley. No way were they going to lock him up in a cage and stick pins in him, or cut bits off him. No tests, no way.

"Give me a colostomy bag and let me go, please!"

"Don't you see, this is going to advance medical science by decades. Imagine, if I can find out what happened, the recognition I could get–"

Eric ran behind the medical bed, pushing it towards the tyrant doctor. He threw a pair of forceps, but the crafty medic deflected them with a practised parry.

"Now, let's not get hasty, Mr. Von Pfeffer. We could work this out together. You might have the answers to life after death, and if you're smart, we could both benefit. If you'll just let me-"

"Forget it! I might be, well, in my current predicament, but I'm still human and humans have rights. I won't have any of this, you amoral fiend. I should've known better than to trust you medical types."

Eric hopped over the unconscious nurse on the floor and made for the exit. But he felt himself snag and with a jerk, pulled back. Looking around, he saw the doctor yank on his dried-out intestines.

"Let me go, please. This isn't fair. Ask yourself if you're being ethical!"

The doctor flashed a patronising smile. "Ethics don't come into play. This is medicine. And what's more, you signed away your life."

He gave a nod towards his desk. Amidst the paperwork, Eric saw a donor card with his own signature, clear on the front. "Or should I add, signed away your life, if you had a life to forfeit," the doctor continued. He tugged on Eric's intestines, and Eric felt himself pulled like a lassoed beast.

There was nothing for it; he had to do self-surgery. He snatched a scalpel off the medical trolley and hacked at his own innards. The leathery intestines broke free. Free! He raced out of the room, down the corridor and out of the hospital.

Freedom of sorts. A strange sensation had overcome his body; actions without feelings. It was liberating, in a sense. He was dead. He didn't have to think about life. He could rethink all the morals that bound him before – good versus bad. Besides, nothing bound him now; he'd been cut free from his own guts. A gutless man could do anything.

***

Eric ran home barefoot. His dried soles slapped on the pavement, making a sound like fists hitting a buffalo-hide punchbag. He felt aware that as he ran, he didn't need to gasp for breath. Those days were behind him. The days of being restricted to earthly turmoil.

This was a new turmoil, he decided. An existential crisis. What was he? Not living, but technically not dead. He had no death certificate and, in fact, didn't even know if he had passed away or not. Maybe he was suffering from a tropical disease? Porphyria?

No, that didn't make sense. He needed to stop all the hypochondria, forget reading the Medical Dictionary at home. It wasn't in his head this time; this was real life. He couldn't have a tropical disease because he hadn't been abroad. Yes, rational explanations first. He couldn't afford a holiday with the move to a new town; Bury St. Morts, out in the countryside of Norfolk. It was supposed to be a fresh start, away from his gold-digging distant relatives in Cheshire, who were after his inheritance money. But all the stress had started a nasty stomach illness. And this doctor; who was he to jump to conclusions like that? Maybe he'd got his medical certificate out of an Easter egg. What sort of small-town hospital doctor made jokes about being dead? That was it, it had to be. He had an illness, a new kind of immunity, like the doctor said. Something living, something alive, that was eating at him. Yes, had to be alive. The thought of anything else killed him. No, no, no! Not killed him. Another word, think, quick. The thought of anything else befuddled him. Yes! That would suffice. No talk of death, killed, dying, anymore – evermore.

The thing the doctor had pulled from him had been a tapeworm, not his intestines. Tapeworms grew to over ten metres in length, wound themselves the whole length of a person's gut. That explained it; that was why he didn't feel any more pain. Stomach problems in the past had been excruciating, but in the doctor's room at the hospital, he had been numb. Now he had an explanation. The tapeworm had caused him pain, and now he was free of it. He was free of his parasite, not his guts.

Eric jogged up his garden path and fumbled in his pocket. He found his key and stuck it in the lock. His fingers jiggled, twisting it. Then there was a crisp snapping sound. A twig breaking? Eric looked down. His index finger lay on the doorstep.

"Oh God – oh Jesus, help!" Eric dropped to his haunches and picked up the offending item, then shoved it in his pocket. He gave a fleeting look to either side, his eyes skirting the living room windows. Had the neighbours seen? Hoped not. He didn't want to get off to a bad start in a new area.

Gotta get inside his house, quick. He was safe. He slammed the door and leaned against it, then forced himself to inhale and exhale. Humans breathed, and he was human. For the time being, he would have to feign normality. Act to fit in, yes, that was the ticket.

He looked in the hallway mirror. His colour was worse than before; a sort of duck-egg blue. Gotta do something about it, at the double. But what?

A-ha! In the bathroom, there was a compact powder. Nina had left it there, right before she had dumped him. The cow was happy to move all her junk into his new pad, and then leave it there once she walked out.

Upstairs he went, taking the steps two at a time. He felt fit and flexible, now that the stomach pain had been alleviated. How could he be dead if he was still energetic? He was thirty-five, in the prime of life. He was simply offish, a bit under the weather because of his gastroenteritis. As he pulled the lid off the compact, Eric ignored the stump of his missing finger. He applied generous amounts of foundation all over his face and neck. The peachy tone on top of his blue skin gave him a greyish hue. Whatever. Grey was better than blue; more natural. Made him blend in better with the English weather, at the very least.

Job done, what now? He felt excitable, hasty. The doctor had got under his skin. His eyes travelled down to his pocket. What about his finger? He needed answers. He had to know what was going on. How? Why? Why him? Why today? He'd just bought his new place and he couldn't even enjoy it. Boy, did it make him cross. Sod's law, for sure.

Answers. So be it. He would have to do a self-autopsy. Eric closed his eyes and shook his head. Not a self-autopsy, a self-examination. Gotta stop with all the negative thinking until he knew for sure. Living until proven dead, not the other way round.

He went downstairs, in a slow, calm and collected manner. How would he do it? Sitting seemed best. If he gave himself a fright, he might faint and that wouldn't do; what if, in his tender condition, he didn't wake up again? He went into the kitchen and found a bread knife in a drawer. The serrated edge would cut well, if he worked it like a saw.

Kitchen chair at the ready. He plonked his ass down and gripped the knife handle with his intact hand. "Here goes nothing," he said. Best start with the existing hole in his stomach. Gentle pressure pried it open, enough to wedge the knife in. No pain, but he'd expected that. He was in shock after all; the pain would set in later as normal. He began to saw. A sound like fabric being cut reached his ears.

No blood, no guts. He lifted back the skin of his stomach and looked in. It was darker than he'd imagined inside his torso. He saw an item that looked like a dried fig dangling from a desiccated branch. A few other organs looked as though they'd been tipped right out of a canopic jar.

Eric heaved and vomited up the dried-fig organ. He picked up the rubbery object and put it back inside. "This isn't happening... this isn't right."

Gotta sew it up. Yes: sew it quick. He had fishing line in another drawer. Didn't have needles, but if he made holes using a nail, he could poke the vinyl line through and pull it tight enough to cover the ghastly hole. He worked as quickly as he could while still being neat. Strange that he felt devoid of emotion as he worked. Was he even capable of emotions anymore? Feelings were human, products of a working brain. He wasn't human. He was a monstrosity.

Negative thoughts, but he couldn't deny it any longer. The doctor said he had no heartbeat. Eric clamped a hand over his own chest. The doctor was right.

He had to face facts. Somehow or other, through some miracle, or the opposite; a perversion of nature, he was alive but dead. Denial wouldn't help him and he needed what he could to help him deal with his unholy fate.

***

The doorbell rang. And rang again, repeatedly and aggressively. Eric rolled out of bed. He'd fallen asleep, or at least drifted off into some vacuous realm of non-existence. What time was it anyway?

Eleven o'clock. Who could be at the door at this hour?

He put on his flannel slippers and went, bleary-eyed, to answer.

A man stood on his doorstep. He was about six foot tall with long, dirty-blonde hair swept into a ponytail under a black baseball cap. He had on a black bomber jacket and black skinny jeans. The bloke's hooded eyes skittered across Eric's face before he fixed Eric with an accusing stare.

"I'm your neighbour from number twenty-three next door and I've been hearing banging and thumping noises for weeks. I just thought I'd tell you, because sometimes people do things that disturb their neighbours and they don't realise it. They need to be told about these annoying things so they can stop."

The shady neighbour jittered on the spot, his hands twitchy and his eyes darting around. Was the bloke on drugs?

"Well, I was having a lie-down, so it couldn't have been me," said Eric.

The bloke's eyes looked ready to pop from his skull. "Look, I'm trying to let you know so you can do something about it, before this thorny situation becomes worse," he said, in a menacing voice.

Thorny situation? What was the guy's problem? He had to be drugged up. Either that or simply psycho. And what a time for a complaint. There were more pressing issues on Eric's mind. Like, how could the bloke not have noticed Eric's obvious physical state? Perhaps it was time to turn on the hallway light, which he'd forgotten to do in his freshly-woken daze, and scare off the guy.

Light on. The sight of Eric's wizened features didn't faze the bloke. The neighbour clenched his jaw, turned on the spot and stormed off without saying anything. Down Eric's garden path, up his own garden path and into his house, slamming the door. Eric heard a string of swear words and banging next door. So, not only was Eric biologically challenged, but he lived next to a loon. What else could go wrong in his afterlife? No rest for the wicked, or so the saying went. Apparently so. Was he suffering for sins committed in his lifetime? But he wasn't religious, didn't even go to church. Though now was as good a time as any to start some soul-searching. Were there other people like him? How had he come to be in his present state? The problems had started since he'd moved to Bury St. Morts. Could it be a problem with a local source? Until he found his answers, he would have to keep a low profile from the medics. The hospital knew about him, but not his address; his assessment had been quick in A&E. Lucky for him that bought him time. But where to start?

His thoughts reverted to the nuisance neighbour, continuing his verbally abusive diatribe while he smashed up his own house in a rage against some imaginary noise. That was it; start with the neighbours. He would ask them if anyone else was feeling under the weather, like himself, in Bury St. Morts.

Eric changed his slippers for shoes and pulled on a jacket; not that he was in any danger of catching his death of cold. He chuckled. Better to laugh than to cry. He had to stay upbeat. Immortality meant forever, so no point dwelling on his misfortunes. He decided he would start with the neighbour on the other side. The street was a cul-de-sac of terraced houses. Maybe they might've noticed something themselves; something in the drinking water, perhaps.

He rang the doorbell of number twenty-seven. A woman answered. "Yes? What the bloody hell is going on? What time of night do you call this to come knocking at someone's door?"

Eric sighed. "As you can see, I don't think the laws of this earthly domain apply to me anymore… in my present condition, that is. Nevertheless, I'm terribly sorry for the intrusion, but I wondered if you'd noticed anything unusual – that is to say – have you had any family illnesses lately?"

The woman scowled at him. "Yes, as a matter of fact. My son is deathly ill in bed. I'm nursing him at the moment. So if you wouldn't mind–"

"Sorry to have disturbed you, I hope he gets well soon," said Eric, with an apologetic wave.

Odd. She hadn't noticed his state of decomposition either. The stranger the situation became, the more Eric felt convinced the locality had something to do with it. The normal responses of his neighbours to his abnormal situation unsettled him. And what of the woman's son? The boy had a mysterious illness, and so did he, Eric with his stomach problems. Then there was the nut-job in twenty-three on the other side, making wild accusations about non-existent noise. Come to think of it, there was a strange ringing in Eric's ears. A word came to mind: tinnitus? Was it to do with the desiccation of his inner ear? Maybe the psycho-neighbour-bloke was hearing things if he too was undergoing his own process of flaccidity.

Eric stood in his hallway in the grip of a brainwave. He was on a mission to get to the bottom of all the devilry. Death had its plus side; time was on his side. He didn't have to concern himself with eating, drinking or sleeping anymore. Bodily functions no longer bothered him. The night was young.

***

Out of his street, around the block and into the local park. To think of going into such a place after dark when he was alive had been inconceivable. But now, what was the worst that could happen to him? He couldn't be killed; he was already dead. He no longer feared knives, dogs, maniacs. Those were all yesterday's worries.

Ahead, he could see two teenage boys in the gloom sitting on a picnic table. Their voices carried on the still air quite easily and Eric caught all of the words.

"You can't say that – you're not black!"

"Why not? You say it."

"But I'm black! Only black people can say the 'N' word."

"But, I was rapping, that's different!"

"Is not!"

"Is too!"

Exasperated voices. Eric got closer. As he neared them, he saw immediately that both boys were clearly, obviously, dead. The nearest one was grey-green and the other looked a waxy yellow in the moonlight.

"Ahem," said Eric. "I don't mean to cut in, but I couldn't help overhearing your conversation. Do you both realise the state you're in?"

The boys stared at him with bulging eyes, their eyelids having receded, fuck-knew when.

"Who asked you to butt in?"

"Normally I wouldn't, but your argument doesn't make sense. Neither of you are black anymore. If anything, you're grass-green and you look like mustard."

"That's not the point," said Greener. "It's the principle of the thing. He's racist."

"Am not! I just rapped, 'what's up my – and then I said the 'n' word as part of the lyrics," said Mustard.

"Exactly. Racist bastard!" shouted Greener.

The boys started cuffing each other. Eric reached between them and pulled them apart, careful not to dislodge any shrivelled limbs in the process.

"Look, don't you get it? Your skin colour has long gone, disappeared. If you want to label each other something, call each other culturalist, not racist. The 'N' word is often used in rapping anyway."

Mustard pointed right at Eric's face. "See? He backs me up, it's cultural, man!"

Eric rolled his eyes skywards. They stuck there and he had to right them with his fingers. "You two really need to sort this out. You might be needing each other more than you think."

"Why?" said Greener. "What for?"

Eric stroked his chin as he thought. "Tell me this, lads, whereabouts do you live?"

"What do you wanna know that for?" said Mustard. "You some sort of paedo?"

"Hardly," Eric scoffed. "If I tried to rape anyone, my dick might be liable to drop off. Look at me."

Silence. He'd clearly got the boys thinking.

"We live in a cul-de-sac over there. Numbers ten and twelve backing onto that field," said greener.

Interesting. Eric stared in the direction of his street. There was something going on in the area for sure. This was deep – as deep as a stiff in a grave plot. And he'd get to the bottom of it, one way or another. He walked home, mulling it all over. In the morning, he would call a street meeting to figure it all out. No doubt about it; there had to be other zombies in his street.

Whether it was in the air, the water, the houses; he'd figure it out.

Funny how the mind worked. Eric grinned at his idle musings. Technically, he was deceased. So how was he able to think? The brain was a physical thing, made of matter. He'd never given much thought to having a soul before, but now nothing else made sense. His body had to be governed by an energy force that steered his necrotic body.

***

It had been a long night, filled with swearing from the psycho neighbour in number twenty-three and coming to terms with the mechanics of his newly deceased body. Not all cons though; the gauntness of his cheeks rather appealed to him. Gone were the days of his fat-faced look. But enough of the superficial twaddle; he needed to be proactive. Got to find out if any other residents in his street had suffered the same fate as Greener and Mustard and himself.

Eric stepped out into the early morning sun. Better skip crackpot twenty-three and start with the other neighbours. He went door to door, knocking at all the houses. A street meeting was a good start; he could get everyone to rally round if need be. Maybe he was being a tad idealistic, but he figured if a hidden devilry was to be uncovered, they all had to band together, work it out.

The neighbours congregated on the street. Some were bemused, some totally mystified and others downright aggrieved.

"Now look here," shouted one particularly desiccated man. "What is the meaning of this harassment?"

"Yes, tell us," said a lady with a bleached-bone complexion. "We thought it was the Michael bloke from number twenty-three." She jerked her bony thumb at the house next to Eric's.

"Oh, I see – so other people have been having trouble with that jumped-up nutcase too?" said Eric.

"Of course. He's the menace of our street," said another stiff, with a rotten tomato skin tone. "But that isn't a concern right now. Tell us what's this all about? We have a right to know."

"Yes, especially when you get us out of bed," shouted a corpulent corpse.

"And it better be good. I'm none too keen on traipsing out in my slippers before I've even had my cornflakes." The woman didn't seem to realise she had no more need for food.

Eric flapped his hands at everyone, motioning for quiet. "Look, I'm sorry to get you all up and about at this ungodly hour. But let's face facts – an ungodly hour is best for ungodly freaks."

Silence as the crowd digested his words.

"Whatever do you mean?" said a voice in the crowd.

Eric continued. "Well, unless you're completely deluded, you may have noticed that everyone in this street has been afflicted with a most monstrous condition."

"Such as?" said the bleached-bone woman.

"Rigor mortis if you want it in technical terms. Dead-as-a-doornail if you care for it straight."

"Doorknob," said the desiccated bloke. "And I don't care for it straight."

"I care for it straight. Damn straight," shouted a woman, who Eric recognised as his neighbour in number twenty-seven. "My boy was ill for days with stomach complaints. He lay down as good as dead last night and when he got up this morning, he was putrid but perky. I hosed him out in the back garden, but the rotting smell won't go away."

A smile spread across his face. "So, you mean, you believe me?"

The woman gave a derisive snort. "Not half! My boy was ill in bed when you called to my house last night, and now he's dead."

"Living dead, to be precise," said Eric. "It's good to focus on the positives at a time like this—"

"I wasn't finished. I was about to say, he died while I had to answer the door to you. This is your fault. I think you're a curse." She pointed a finger at him, her narrowed eyes full of hatred.

Eric shook his head. "Now, let's not be hasty. You're just irritable because you're deceased. It's no reason to take it out on other people."

"Wait a minute," said the desiccated man. "I started feeling ill a few weeks ago around the time your moving van came into the street. She must be right."

"Listen, we shouldn't argue. We'll be stuck with each other for infinity, so maybe we should rally round, try to get along," said Eric.

"Don't listen to him, he's evil," shouted the woman from twenty-seven.

"Yes, let's get him," yelled the desiccated man.

"What?" Eric cried. "No, wait, that's not what I meant by rally round."

The residents raised their bony fists. They reached for Eric, snatching handfuls of his clothing. Everyone's blood was up; or would have been if it hadn't coagulated. Eric broke free of their grasps and bolted.

How would he get to the bottom of it now? Not very well, when he was running for his life. Death. Running for his death.

Hold on a minute; why was he running? He was dead. They couldn't hurt him. What was the worst that could happen? He reached the field at the end of the street and stopped, leaning against the fence.

The crowd caught up. Bony hands clawed at him as they grabbed his torso. Gnarled fingers delved inside the gash in his stomach and hooked around his ribcage. They shoved him over the fence and climbed behind him as he fell, face first into a pool of mud. A few walking corpses slipped into the mud pool with him, their bodies clumsy with rigor mortis.

"Tie him up with the scarecrow," a resident yelled.

Eric was lifted up. Six of them held him high like pallbearers. If only he really were dead. So much for the afterlife. If he'd known it was going to be this much hassle, he'd have taken better care of his health. Blasted tummy troubles had caused him no end of bother.

The crowd bound his wrists and ankles to the scarecrow post using shoelaces and belts. What was it to be? Crucifixion? Left as a feast for the birds? "Listen, this doesn't make sense. Don't you get it? I'm dead, you're dead, we're all in this together. Can't we work this thing out in a civilised manner?"

"Civilised?" said a man. "I'll give you civilised." He pulled a small silver flask from his inside pocket. Once he'd tipped the contents over the scarecrow, he lit it with a match. Soon the straw had caught fire and Eric went up in flames like a Sunny Jim firelighter. The crowd watched, satisfied, until the flames licked high, before turning to leave.

Eric sighed. Nothing for it but to wait it out. After a long stint of boredom, the fire died down without spreading, as the area around the scarecrow had been cleared. Eric looked down at his body. His clothes had burned away, but he didn't care. He had no need for modesty in his decomposed state. His bonds had burned away too. Freedom. He tried to move, but found that he was stiff... in more than one sense of the word.

"What the-?"

The mud had baked, rock-solid. He had been fired, like a figurine in a kiln. Eric tried to walk, but instead the forward motion made him fall flat on his front. He lay face down in the soil, a useless clay statue.

"This is the pits," he said in a muffled voice.

What would become of him now? He'd end up buried in the soil after a rainstorm came and probably lie there for decades, maybe even centuries, wallowing in self-pity, no doubt.

***

Sunset came and went. As darkness fell, a woman's voice, singing out of tune, met Eric's ears. It grew louder and Eric knew she was approaching. He could also tell, whoever she was, she was drunk. He tried to crane his neck, but it wouldn't budge. His nose stuck in the earth, his baked arms pointing pathetically to either side.

The singing stopped. "Oh? What's this?"

Eric felt hands on his shoulders. The woman groaned as she struggled to tip him over. He felt himself pulled onto one side, so that his weight balanced on his right hand, his left hand oriented skywards and the side of his right foot dug into the soil. The woman appeared below him. Her straggled hair hung limp across her face, shielding her features from him, but from the look of her clothes; a denim jacket and a short floral summer dress, she was youngish. She put both hands on his chest, her face near enough for Eric to smell whisky on her breath. She shoved hard and he flipped over, landing on his back with a thump. He hoped the fall would've broken his clay joints, but the soil was soft and spongy underneath.

"Well, hello there. Fancy meeting such a handsome man here of all places."

Eric tried to speak, but his mud-baked lips were fired shut. Did he hear her right? Handsome? What was going on? Was she too drunk to notice his condition? Or maybe she couldn't see him in the semi-darkness of pre-dawn.

"What a catch," she went on, her words slurred. She stood over him, her legs on either side of his torso. And then she lifted her summer dress. Eric watched her slide her underwear down and step out of it, kicking the knickers to one side.

"Oh no," Eric tried to say, but his jaw wouldn't move. "Not this-"

The woman squatted down and sat back on Eric's hips. "What a night for blow-up Bob to get a puncture – but you'll do just as well," she said. She rocked herself back and forth, her hair flinging across her face. Eric felt mortified. First, he'd been victimised, then burned at the stake, and now violated by a perverted drunk. This was hell for sure. Did he even have a dick anymore? It had probably dried out like the rest of him and now lay caked in mud. Course, that was most likely enough for the kinky bitch on top of him. A hard protuberance that she could thrust herself at would suffice for a person accustomed to the service of inflatable men.

Eric rocked about in the soil, buffeted in misery. Might've been nice if he could actually have felt anything, but his mud casing sealed him in like a concrete condom. The woman shifted herself and used his splayed clay fingers to pleasure herself. In and out, in and out, incessantly, degradingly. When would a rainstorm come to wash him clean?

After she had satisfied herself, the woman stood up and smoothed down her dress. She scooped up her knickers and stuffed them in one of the pockets of her denim jacket. "Well, that was a fine treat, Pottery-Pete. I hope to see you again tonight, lover."

And she was off. Mercy indeed. Eric needed to break himself, quick. He needed to crack his joints so that he could run away. There was no way he could endure another night of humiliation. No more tonights, tomorrows, or ever-afters, ever again. *Lover.* Insult to injury, it was!

***

Morning light came, a grey dawn to match his troubled soul; if only he had one. Faint voices reached him on the breeze. Not the woman again, please, anything but her...

Two men appeared, carrying metal detectors. What luck. Now he stood a chance of freedom. He watched them come closer through the hay, until with a clunk, a metal detector hit his ribcage.

"Woah, what's that there?" said one man.

"Blimey. Beats me," said the other.

"That some sorta scarecrow, do you reckon?"

"Nah, couldn't be. It's some kinda artefact. Told you there was loads of ancient stuff round here. Probably Viking, or even Celtic."

"Yeah, but where's the Roman coins. I don't want no mummy - or whatever the hell that thing is."

"Don't write it off so quickly. It could be the next Sutton Hoo."

"Sutton what?"

"Viking ship burial. There was gold and all sorts of treasure found with the body."

"Well, where's the gold? Where's the ship?"

Silence. Eric watched the two men as they pondered him.

"Let's take him to the Bury St. Morts Archaeological Conservation Trust. They'll know what to do. Never know, we might get a mint out of this."

The men turned and left. Eric watched them until they disappeared. An eternity later in his lonely patch of field, he heard them return. One had a coil of rope over his shoulder. They tied it around his chest, under his armpits and dragged him towards the fence. With a bump, Eric felt himself loaded onto the back of a truck. As the truck trundled along, trees passed and Eric tried not to feel nauseous. Could he still get travel sick, or was it merely psychosomatic? Who knew? Maybe there'd be a decent scientist at the Bury St. Morts Archaeological Conservation Trust who could analyse him and figure things out.

***

The two Archaeologists peered down at Eric on the table. There was a large man in his mid-thirties with slick, black hair plastered flat on his head. His eyes were magnified by spectacles with lenses as thick as glass bottle bottoms. His twenty-something female assistant had long bushy brown hair and a brow that furrowed into a single line as she observed Eric with disgust.

"This is unusual," said the man. "Most unusual indeed. Pity they didn't find him in situ. I could've had a team out there digging."

Eric rolled his eyes sideways to survey the basement office where he now lay on a mortuary-slab of a table. There were shelves full of chemicals and broken relics that had been there for fuck-knew how long. Would he too end up another relic on a shelf? Or donated to a museum? The so-called experts seemed as incompetent as the doctor who had examined him at hospital. But no, he couldn't be too hard on them. His circumstances were hitherto unheard of. He and the residents of his street were ecological wonders, walking miracles.

"It doesn't look to be a sarcophagus," said the woman. "You don't think there could be a body inside, do you, Moe?"

The man, Moe, stroked his chin. "The X-ray should show that later. But no, I would say this is an artefact of human manufacture designed as a sacrificial offering. Gimme a torch there, Eunice. I want to have a closer look."

"Look at the intricate designs on his buckle, the interweaving lattice. I'd say this effigy dates from the early Christian period, maybe even before," said Eunice, passing him a flashlight.

Moe looked to be concentrating so hard, he didn't notice dropping cigarette ash on Eric. "No, this is definitely earlier. That's a Celtic symbol. I'd say this is an Iron Age artefact."

Eric recalled the Gaelic design on his belt. He'd got it for eight quid in Asda.

"But the style of the object, not to mention the size–" said Eunice.

"Eunice, don't you have enough to be getting on with? I gave you those papers to proof-read for me; have you done that?" said Moe, looking down his nose at her.

"Yes." Eunice sighed. "I made the grammatical corrections and rewrote some parts for you."

"Good. Then why don't you get back to work on Sir Baal's coffin. Treating the delicate casing is cryptic work, is it not? Get it? Cryptic?" Moe snorted, waiting for Eunice to laugh too, but before she could respond, the Indiana Jones theme tune blared.

"You'd better get the phone," she said in a dry tone.

Footsteps as Eunice walked away. Moe's generous gut perched on Eric's torso as he pored over him. Eric tried to not let it distract him as he listened to the phone call.

Moe grabbed the phone. "Bury St. Morts Archaeological Conservation Trust, Head of Conservation, Moe Lester speaking. Can I help you?"

A tremor rocked Eric as a giggle, suppressed by his mud-encasement surged through his body. Was the Head of archaeological conservation seriously called molester?

Eric stared at the ceiling, the laughter subsiding. How long would he be stuck with the Archaeological Conservators? More to the point, how long before they figured out he was animated. It all seemed like a huge joke. Pretentious talk from pseudo-scientists; Iron Age, intricate designs. And what of this idiot, Moe Lester? He bustled about at the other end of the basement office, out of sight. Eric could hear him humming the Indiana Jones theme tune. Corny and clichéd, fitting the stereotype to a capital S. And what of the man contaminating his own artefacts with cigarette ash? It seemed like sloppy work.

Eric heard the phone click and saw Eunice stride back into view. Moe took a large book off a shelf and flicked through it, then jabbed his finger at a page.

"Look, Eunice. See here? This is an offering that was found in the Thames when they dredged in the seventies. Notice the similarities between the La Tene style of this picture with our guy here. He even has the same crude facial features."

Crude? Eric felt a tremor of anger. Crude, indeed. The bloke had a nerve – he was no looker himself.

"But, what we have here is the same Iron Age offering on a life-size scale. This is a unique find. I'll bet my left bollock it's the only one of its kind in the whole of the UK." Moe paced around Eric in a flurry of excitement. "In fact, I have a new proposal. I want you to suspend all work on Sir Harry Baal's coffin for the time being. You can get yourself a drawing board and make me some artistic representations of this sacrificial offering. I'm going to write an article for Archaeology Today magazine. I'll need some illustrations to go in the Journal with my write-up."

Harry Baal. Another tremor rippled through Eric as a tsunami snigger overcame his body. Hairy Ball, indeed. It sounded like such a fabricated name.

Moe strode over to his desk and sat down. He pulled a paper pad towards him and began to write. Eunice pulled a chair close to Eric and sat with a drawing board perched on her knee. She stared intently at Eric, before plotting a few points on the tracing paper that overlaid the grid-lined board. Then she began to sketch, with her head down. Eric looked back to Moe. He could see the bespectacled man's reflection in the metallic pipes that ran across the basement office ceiling. Moe wasn't writing an article. He was doing a sketch that at first glance appeared to be a catapult. Eric studied it. The drawing had been labelled, with arrows running out to the edges, where Moe had described parts of the diagram in detail. The picture seemed familiar. Eric thought hard. He'd seen it before in a sci-fi movie; Back to the Future. It was the flux capacitor.

Ha! So the so-called head Archaeological Conservator sat doodling and let his assistant do all the work. The woman probably put up with him for extra credit. She'd probably even end up writing the article too, all for Moe Lester to stick his name on the top. These pseudo-academics were nothing more than charlatans, out to change history into a quick ego-fix.

It was the final straw for Eric; he rumbled with laughter inside his rigid casing. His body spasmed within the baked mud shell and he felt himself rock on the table. The motion reached a crescendo as his body succumbed to laughter. He rolled from side to side and slipped closer and closer to the edge of the table. Eunice didn't look up, busy with her sketching.

With a crack, Eric hit the floor. Eunice yelped and jumped up. Her drawing board hit the floor with a clatter. He'd done it; he'd broken loose. His neck and shoulder joints were free. The mud had cracked off his midriff, allowing him to sit up. Eunice screamed and threw her hands over her face as Eric got to his knees. Moe, who was also on his feet, stared. His ruddy face had turned pale and blotchy. Without a word he raced up the stairs, out of his basement office, leaving Eunice in hysterics.

Eric put his hands up in an open gesture. "Please, Miss, don't be afraid. It's not what it seems." His words did not have the intended affect. Eunice stopped screaming, her face frozen in fear. She staggered back, bumping against her desk, without taking her eyes off Eric. Then she turned and bolted out of the basement office too.

Oh well. Eric had long since resigned himself to the fact that he wouldn't get any help from supposed professionals. But at least they'd done him a favour by making him laugh. His limbs had been freed.

***

Eric got the bus back from the Bury St. Morts Archaeological Conservation Trust. He wasn't sure exactly where he was, other than in the depths of Suffolk's countryside. Fortune was on his side for once, as the bus driver didn't give him a second glance. He'd gotten most of the largest chunks of baked mud off his body, but still, it would've been an unpleasant walk for days to get back to Bury St. Morts in Norwich, from somewhere that he guessed was vaguely near Southwold beach. The passing view of the sea calmed him as the bus weaved a scenic coastal route until it turned inland and was swallowed by hedgerows and trees.

He must've looked a frightful sight. Misshapen pottery lumps dangled from his elbows and knees like Christmas ornaments on a grotesque tree. How long had it been since he'd seen his reflection? Not that he cared to anymore; his state of decomposition would definitely be stomach churning. But then he remembered; he no longer had any internal organs. His gastric reflux days were long gone. Eric felt sad. How nice it would be to suffer bodily malfunctions once more.

The bus dropped him off at Cambridge bus station and he bought a ticket from the machine back to Norwich. Nobody among the morning commuters gave him a fleeting glance. It made sense; he looked like a vagrant, and where more than Cambridge had a bigger problem of homeless drifters. Eric muttered to himself as he walked onto the platform. Let them think he was mentally ill too, or on drugs; that would keep any curious eyes from resting on him. He'd blend in properly with the crowd.

The train pulled up and Eric took a seat tucked away in a corner. A newspaper had been left on the seat next to him and he used it to cover his face. With a bit of luck, people would think him asleep and leave him alone until his stop. Eric looked out the window from under his newspaper as the train whizzed north, his mind full of thoughts. Would his neighbours have realised by now that he wasn't the cause of the epidemic in the street? Had the disease of living dead perhaps spread to other streets in the time he had left? The train slowed as it pulled into Ely. Outside lay stretches of fens; reclaimed land that had once been swamp. Could the disease have been transmitted by mosquitos living out in the marshes? He didn't recall having been bitten by a bug, nor did Bury St. Morts lie near any fens. If anything, it was close to The Wash, near the coast of Norfolk. But if not a plague, then what? Viruses, bacteria, anthrax; it was all stuff of Hollywood, not real life. This was a biological conundrum that was linked to his hometown and nowhere else. His doctor in hospital couldn't figure it out; even the scientists at the conservation trust hadn't picked up on the truth of it all. Maybe he had as much of a shot at it as anyone.

They arrived in Kings Lynn with a bump. The newspaper toppled off Eric's face and landed on his knee. His eyes fell on the front page headline, and widened: *Archaeologists uncover evidence of Druid magic in the British Isles.* He skimmed the article, key phrases jumping out at him from the text. *Celtic artefact. Terracotta effigy. The first of its kind in the UK. Lifesize figurine in La Tene style, suggesting it most likely served as an offering to Iron Age gods. X-ray showed no evidence of organic matter inside. Thermoluminescent dating provided a rough estimation of construction around 500 BC.*

Ha! What a laugh. Seemed Moe Lester had overcompensated for having lost his prized find. These archaeological conservators, or whatever they were, were only good at conserving their egos and academic reputations. Still, Eric marvelled at how quickly they had got word out to the papers.

Druid magic. Did magic exist? Anything seemed possible after what had happened to him. Could it be a sort of magic, propelling him? A voodoo curse, like those zombies working the fields in Haiti? Although, those people in Haiti weren't actually dead; simply drugged. Their purpose was to work as slaves, according to a TV documentary, at least. Did he, Eric, have a purpose? Existing on earth forever, not alive but not dead, counted as a kind of slavery he supposed. Maybe being poisoned to work for an evil overlord was a worse fate. Unlike the Haitian zombies, he had his own free will. Everything he did was for the good of himself and the people of his village. Not that they deserved it, of course, for burning him at the stake.

Witchcraft. It was as likely as plagues or mutations, any of the numerous nasty reasons that came to mind. Occam's Razor. He had to get back to basics and find the simplest explanation. The train slowed at Norwich. Eric threw the newspaper in the bin and got off.

***

"So, what can I call you?"

Eric stared at the woman in number twenty-seven before answering. He felt awkward enough sitting in her living room, without the accusatory tone on top of things.

"My name's Eric ran... ran..."

"Yes?" she encouraged.

"It's no use. I can't say it. Do you have something to write on?"

She handed him a notepad and pen. He scribbled his name and held it up.

"Eric Von Pfeffer," she read. "Why won't you say it? Is it because you're all over the papers? You must want to stay anonymous."

Eric shook his head. "No, they don't know my name. That wasn't me in the paper anyway – that was some sculpture they built to look like me."

The woman smiled. "Your name has a nice ring to it. You should be proud of it."

"It's not that." He pointed to his receding lip, the flesh curled back from his teeth.

"Oh, I see," she said. "You can't say V's or P's. Eric Von Pfeffer. I guess it's a mouthful."

Eric nodded solemnly.

"I suppose I don't have long myself before my bits and bobs dry out too," said the woman, in a surprisingly upbeat voice. "My son died before me and his thingy-ma-jigs are falling off willy-nilly." She clapped a hand over her mouth, looking embarrassed. "Oops - bad pun. He was ever so upset about the loss of his pee-pee. He hates feeling emasculated. He was barely hitting puberty – it's a lot for a boy of that age to take."

Eric thought of the night he'd called to her house. She'd been busy nursing her son as he had convalesced. Poor tyke. "Where is he today anyway?"

"He's at church with most of the street. They're praying for a miracle."

"Do they all realise it was nothing to do with me?"

She nodded. "After we burned you in the field–" She hung her head. "I'm most awfully sorry about that–"

Eric waved her apology off. "Not a problem. At least it didn't hurt me."

"Anyway, the deaths kept happening, so we knew it couldn't be you, as we thought you were gone. Everyone was on edge as you can imagine, so we were looking to pin it on the first thing that went wrong. And it just happened that Michael, that bloke on the other side of you, kicked off at the wrong moment – for him."

"What happened?" Eric sat forward. "What did he do?"

"He banged on the door of the people in number twenty-one, ranting about noise. They're a lovely young couple, you know, decent folks. Anyway, he accused the lady of walking up and down on her wooden living room floor in high heels, saying the clacking sound was keeping him up at all hours. They got into a fight cos she said she didn't own high heels, didn't even have a wooden floor, but he wouldn't listen, shouting and swearing like a lunatic. You wouldn't believe how long that menace has been intimidating the whole street. And that wasn't all – we finally got proof."

"Proof of what – or do I want to know?" said Eric.

"The couple in twenty-one saw him out their back window dealing drugs to two of the boys who live round the next street. I think they live in numbers ten and twelve."

Greener and Mustard. The crackpot in twenty-three was a drug dealer; and judging by his wild accusations of imaginary noise, using his own supplies himself.

"So, did the couple do something?"

"Yes, along with the other neighbours in our street. They got into a fist fight in the road, and when they realised that Michael had a healthy glow, unlike the rest of us, they thought he was a witch behind all the deaths. Course, now in hindsight, we realise he was using acrylic paint on his face to cover the truth – he was actually dying like the rest of us."

Eric tried not to smile. "What did they do to him?"

"They threw him into the boot of a car and drove him right into the centre of Norwich. They took him to the top of Norwich Cathedral and impaled him on one of the spires."

Eric couldn't hold in his laughter. "Why Norwich Cathedral?"

She shrugged. "It's the symbol of Norfolk, isn't it? We hoped the death plague afflicting us all would have gone away after that, but it didn't. I guess Michael was just another scapegoat in the end, like you."

"Is he still up there?"

She shook her head. "They took him down before daylight. He was subdued after that. Been quiet in his house ever since. Finally, now we might have a bit of respite in our afterlife."

"But we still don't know what's happening," said Eric, a desperate note in his voice.

"I know. That's why we're taking a leaf out of your book. I'm calling a street meeting," she answered.

"Oh, so that's why you stuck an invite to come over through my door. I wondered why you would want me to come for tea and cake when neither of us have the need for food and drinks anymore." Eric sighed. Couldn't have been a come-on either, since neither of them had a need for sex anymore.

The doorbell rang and the woman went to answer. A few of the street's residents came in. Eric saw among them Michael, finally cowed.

"Eric," said one of the men, his head lowered. "Sorry about the burning. No hard feelings, eh?"

"Yeah, er, sorry," said a woman behind him.

"You're kinda famous now," said a teenage boy. Eric recognised Greener from the park. He was now a deep khaki shade and a few loose skin flaps hung from his cheeks.

"Eric the Effigy, they're calling you," said another kid, and Eric rested his eyes on Mustard, Greener's friend. He looked like a wax dummy, his skin the colour of autumn hay.

"Yeah," said their host, the woman from twenty-seven. "Nicknames stick. Eric the Effigy and Spikey Mikey."

Everyone laughed but crackpot twenty-three, Michael, scowled.

"Go ahead, laugh," growled Michael. "How would you like to be stuck at the top of that spire?"

One of the men cackled. "We always did think you had a pole up your keister!"

"You're all being unfair to me," Michael wailed, his Adam's apple wobbling. "As if I haven't suffered enough retribution." He showed a letter. Eric stole a glance and caught the first part:

Dear Mr. Michael Alexander, Due to complaints from your neighbours regarding ongoing noise and nuisance issues, and a breach of your contract at number twenty-three owing to the possession and storage of illegal narcotics on said premises, we regret to inform you that your tenancy agreement will be terminated with two months' notice to vacate the premises on May 1st.

"Did you see that? Just where do they get off on these lies upon lies. Where am I going to live now? Who will rent to me in this unpresentable state?"

"Well, I think you got what you deserved for making all our lives hell and for dealing drugs to teenagers. Shame on you," said the woman from number twenty-one.

"Yes, we don't need a nuisance neighbour especially now that we're all going to be together forever it seems, whether you get evicted or not," said the woman from twenty-seven.

"In fact, isn't getting together why we came?" said another man from their street. He looked at Eric. "You mentioned before that you wanted to rally together. Do you know something we don't about our situation?"

Eric shook his head. "Afraid not. But maybe we can all start piecing this thing together. There's got to be some logic, right? So, let's think about it. When did you all notice your symptoms starting? An illness, an accident; it must've started with a traceable event."

"Well," said the woman in twenty-seven, "In my case, I noticed I was feeling unwell after I picked some blackberries from the field at the end of the street. I made a pie and it must've given me and my son food poisoning. He got sick first, probably because he's so young. We got worse and worse until the pain just went away. But we had no feeling either and I noticed we were both a funny colour. We've been getting worse as the days go on and bits have been, well, you know what I mean – dropping off and such."

"As for me," said a man, "I was out gardening and I must've got a cut. Next thing I knew, it was infected. At first, it got septic, and I was feverish but then, just as she said, I got better suddenly. There was no pain. The infection didn't go away, but it stopped spreading and didn't hurt, though my colour became offish." He lifted his trouser leg and showed a ragged patch of skin that looked like it had once been rotten, but had now dried out."

Eric thought of his own situation; stomach pain that had worsened after the move. He'd thought it was IBS from the stress, or maybe food poisoning. But now–

He jumped to his feet. "I think I might've found a pattern. Tell me more – how did you boys die?"

Greener shrugged. "Nothing happened to us. We were just mucking about in the park by the field. We didn't have no accident, or nothing."

Hmm. The field by the park. The field that bordered their street. All of the cases seemed to be linked to the environment in one way or another. "I wonder... But I need to find out more," said Eric.

"What is it?" asked the woman in twenty-seven.

"Well, I've heard of babies being born deformed if they live near a nuclear power plant, or through asbestos. Or even if there are pesticides being used in neighbouring fields. And it makes me think… I wonder if such pollutants could make people die, I mean, without dying. Without even noticing."

Michael from twenty-three stood up. "Well, if you ask me, I'd say that all this is caused by only one thing."

The woman from twenty-seven glowered at him. "And what would that be, your royal highness?"

Spikey Mikey bristled. "Noise pollution, what else?"

**

"So, Mr. Von Pfeffer, how do you feel now that you've uncovered the illegal use of organophosphate pesticide as the cause of genetic mutation among the villagers of Bury St. Morts?"

Eric looked at the vivacious reporter, envying her life essence. No chance of ever meeting a beautiful woman like her in his state. "Not much, really. As you know, being dead has its setbacks. I don't feel anything much anymore. I suppose the pesticide doesn't affect me now. How could it? I have no more cholinesterase enzyme left in my body to mutate so I guess it's all redundant."

"I understand the residents are trying to get compensation for all the living deaths. How does that work?"

"The short answer is it doesn't. Insurance claims are void if you aren't alive. We aren't eligible. That's why we're protesting today. It's been one month of tireless research and campaigning for us to be kicked to the kerb like this. One month too long."

"But all of your symptoms – you and everyone else in the village – leading up to your deaths, fits all the criteria for pesticide poisoning. It's a textbook perfect case."

"Yes, you would think so and we told them that too." Eric struggled to contain the note of exasperation in his voice. "Abdominal cramps, diarrhoea, slow heartbeat leading to death. But the bottom line is, you have to be alive to get anything done these days. They simply don't cater to the needs of the chronically deceased. It's discrimination, but who said life – I mean, death – was fair?"

"Well, I can certainly say that your resolve is great and your cause an important one." The reporter flashed a healthy grin. "And I can see that your poster has COSHH 1986 written on it. Could you explain for the viewers what that means?"

"The control of substances hazardous to health." Eric rolled the words off his desiccated tongue. "We know the law. We know our rights. And we're campaigning not just for ourselves, but for the rights of the terminally dead everywhere who find themselves getting stiffed by the government - literally and figuratively."

"Finally, Mr. Von Pfeffer, could I ask you what your plans might be once all the press surrounding your claim has died down – excuse the pun."

Eric waved her apology away. "No offence taken. To be honest, I haven't thought further than lobbying to make sure my fellow biologically challenged neighbours and I will not be taken advantage of, either as subjects of scientific experiments, or through discriminatory practices, such as insurance policy loopholes to overlook the needs of zombified people."

The reporter shook Eric's hand. "Thank you for an informative and most interesting interview, Mr. Von Pfeffer. I wish you the best of success with your campaign."

Eric watched the reporter turn to talk to the camera, with a wide grin on her face. He felt empty, before remembering that inside, of course, he was nothing but a hollow body cavity. The reporter had been charming and professional, yet artificial. Who was a more fake human being; her or him? He was an empty husk of a person, stripped of intestines and devoid of long-since vomited-up organs, but at least he had humanity. She was full of wind; empty words. He was full of wind, but he also stood for a cause.

"Ahem."

Eric turned to see a man in a suit standing behind him, looking rather stern.

"Hello, Mr. Von Pfeffer. My name's Jasper Morris. I'm the director of Mean'n'Green Chemicals Incorporated. I understand you're at the centre of this protest?"

"Yes, that would be correct," said Eric in a firm voice.

"Well, I don't much like all this bad publicity my company has been getting at the hands of you – of you zombies."

"Hmph." Eric fought the urge to slug the bloke in the chops, only for fear that his fist might snap off. "And we wouldn't be zombies if it wasn't for you."

Jasper made a derisive grunt. "Arguments aside, I have a proposal which may be of interest to you. And you might want to consider it carefully, given the nature of your, shall we say, circumstances."

Eric stared at the man. "What are you getting at?"

"What I mean to say is, we have a position open for assistant manager in the department of quality control. Our appointee in that particular area is on an extended period of compassionate leave as of this morning, citing stress, after he read all the bad press. I'd be delighted to offer the job to you."

"Why me?"

"You've suffered first hand because of the mutation your cholinesterase enzyme underwent as a result of our new line of organophosphate pesticides. It would help to have your expertise on the team."

Eric held his chin high. "What are the working hours?"

Jasper gave a forced grin. "Well, we were thinking that since you're deceased, you might not fatigue like the others and would therefore be able to put in a good, say, seventy-hour week?"

Eric sneered. "I see. And how much could I expect to be paid for such an undertaking?"

Jasper hesitated. "That's another thing. We surmised that since you no longer have the needs of a regular person, that you could do without the money. In return we could offer you a comfortable office and much to do to stave off those long, lonely hours that no doubt lie ahead for you."

Eric couldn't believe his ears – or rather, the earholes that remained after his lobes had fallen off. "If I wasn't already dead, I would say that I'd rather die than work as slave labour for such a corrupt company run by an amoral person lacking any decent human principles. If you wanted to entice me into not shaming your firm, you could've at least offered me a cash bribe. Money talks and bullshit walks. I could do with the funding to start a charity helping the victims of organophosphate poisoning – it would be a much better use of my afterlife."

The audacity. Eric turned away, leaving Jasper to the taunts of the other protestors. Through the crowd, he saw a blonde-head making a path towards him. Nina, his ex.

"Hello, Eric."

She was as radiant as ever. A pang of sadness overcame him. They could never – he could never – it could never be. She was wearing a denim jacket and a short, floral summer dress. Her style looked different from when they'd dated, yet it seemed familiar. How? Where?

"What do you want, Nina? Your make-up? It's all used up." He pointed to his peachy complexion.

"It's not that. When we broke up it was because, well, the time wasn't right, you know? You weren't serious enough. Neurotic, yes. A hypochondriac, sure. But you weren't doing anything real with your life."

Eric laughed. "Neurotic? Necrotic, more like. And as for doing something real with my life, that'll never happen. Honey, I'm dead. So, what's your point? Did you come to gloat over my misfortune?"

She looked pained, as though she was struggling to say what was on her mind. "The thing is, I like stiff guys and now, well there's nothing more stiff than you."

Eric didn't know whether to laugh or cry. "Sweetie, I'm dead. You could do better. We could never have kids, never mind grow old together. I couldn't even make myself useful around the house in case something dropped off."

Nina shook her head. "You don't understand. I'm into kinky things, like I mean, stuff I didn't tell you about before in case you dumped me. But one night when I was getting my fix in the field at the back of your street—"

His eyes widened. "So, it was you! It was you all along who had sex on me. You dirty little devil."

She blushed. "Yes. I found out later that it was you when that story came out in the Bury St. Morts Newsletter. And this too—" She showed him a journal: *Archaeology Today*. Inside, he saw an article entitled, *Iron Age sacrificial offerings in Bury St. Morts*, written by Moe Lester. At the bottom was an illustration of a life-sized, clay-encrusted figurine, bulky and hideous. Was that really what he had looked like in terracotta? No time for vanity though. He recalled Lester's lackey, Eunice, sketching in the basement laboratory. His eyes skimmed the drawing credit at the bottom: *illustration by Moe Lester*. So, Moe had ripped-off his assistant's work. Typical charlatan; a ladder-climbing fraud.

"See? You're a famous artefact. I've never felt so proud." Nina planted a smacker on what was left of his lips.

Eric closed his eyes, trying to savour the kiss that he couldn't feel. "Nina, you know I love you, but this is all too fast. A few weeks ago I was dying for you to have me back – excuse the pun – but now, I'm telling you to do something better with your life."

He pushed her away gently, but Nina stood her ground. "No. I've something to show you." She put her hands on the rim of her shirt and started to lift it, exposing her midriff.

Oh no; was she pregnant? He reeled. How would he look after a baby? Would the decay be harmful to a child? On the other hand, he'd exist long enough to see it grow up, which was a plus, though then again–

He stared at her belly. No bump. Then what?

Instead of a bump, he noticed a blue-green patch of decayed tissue above her navel.

"I'm dying too. My frolick with you in the field that night was enough to do it. I got exposed to a high dose of that organophosphate pesticide." She threw her arms around him. "Oh Eric, we'll be together forever!"

***

"Nothing on the telly as usual." Eric clicked the remote to turn the TV off and tossed the plastic device on the sofa. "What good's eternity if I have to suffer this BBC rot?"

"Choice words." Nina grinned. She sat down next to him with a plate of cucumber sarnies.

"Oh honey, you shouldn't have." Eric picked up a triangle and nibbled on it. "What's the point?"

Nina shrugged. "If we're going to live like humans, we might as well keep up the pretence. What else would we spend our huge payout from Mean'n'green Chemicals Incorporated on? It's good to keep up the old habits."

Eric swallowed his bite of sandwich and reached into the cavity in his abdomen to pull out the masticated bread. He tossed it in the bin. "Everyone else is doing something with their afterlife, except us. Greener and Mustard have become felons. They've been robbing every town from Cambridge to King's Lynn as a duo called YOLO – You Only Live Once. Best dressed teenagers in Bury St. Morts. And the woman from twenty-seven has been selling her story to all the women's gossip mags, they're lapping it up. Even that drug dealer, Spikey Mikey, has kept himself busy with it all."

"What did he do?" asked Nina.

"He got himself a metal detector and started tearing up the pesticide field for Roman coins while it was closed off for investigation. I heard he registered as the director of a company set up to sell the coins to private collectors abroad. A bloke at the post office told me he was working with Moe Lester from the Bury St. Morts Archaeological Conservation Trust, but they were doing dodgy dealings – apparently if you find artefacts on public land, you're supposed to call a finds liaison officer first. Anyway, they made a mint in a few months, but when they got found out, Moe Lester blamed the lot on Spikey Mikey and it's all going to court soon. So, his numismatic company went bust. He's bankrupt. But not before he dragged Moe into the court case."

"That's awful," said Nina.

Eric shrugged. "Serves them both right if you ask me. Still, it gets you thinking. In six months since the protest, what's happening with our charity? Nobody cares about the plight of the living-dead. They'd rather we go away and haunt a graveyard than bother them with our cause."

Nina squeezed his shoulder. "Don't worry, honey, we have our whole death to think about it."

"Exactly." Eric sat back with a sigh. "But in the meantime, we need to make good use of our time. We can't have kids – and that's something that half the nation does just to fill a gap of boredom in their lives. We can't adopt because technically our decomposition could pose hazardous to a youngster."

"We could get a pet?"

"Not really. Don't you remember the mischief that happened when Spotty from down the street ran off with my femur? Bloody hard to get it back after the little bastard buried it in his back yard."

Nina chewed a cucumber sarnie. "I'm happy to stay home cooking and eating. Think about it – you've bought this house, so they can't kick us out. We don't have to work if we don't want to, because we're dead, and even so, we have our compensation payout to get by on. I can eat all I want and not ever worry about getting fat. Clothes sit better on me now too. If only I'd kept my looks, I could have been a model."

Eric rolled his eyes. "Could've-beens are no good to us. We need constructive ideas, practical plans. We can't stay here all day, every day. It's boring!"

She puckered her mouth, thinking. "I might become a Druid. I've always wanted to get into paganism, and who better than me could sit all night waiting to worship the midwinter dawn without getting tired than the living-dead. I could become a shaman at Seahenge, invoking the ancient goddesses of Celtic Norfolk."

Eric smiled. "I'm impressed – that's not a bad thought. I'd like to do something to help people too. But not by becoming a Druid, or a criminal like those teens. I'm not alive, but still, I'm not above the law."

"What were you thinking then, baby?"

"I dunno. I don't fancy selling my story to magazines either, like the woman in twenty-seven, but she did give me an idea. I might become a writer. It's a job that doesn't need money to start up, but does need time, and I have all the time in the world. Plus, unlike other areas of showbiz like acting or modelling, writing doesn't discriminate about appearances. It wouldn't matter a bit that I'm dead. In fact, it might even help my sales, you know, add a bit of intrigue."

"That's true. If ex-cons and psychos can get their writing on shelves, why not you? There's always an audience for a good read." Nina munched on her sarnie.

"I could write a damn good book, a memoir. Just think what I could tell people – all about my experience, starting from my stomach problems and my diagnosis of death. I'd write under a pseudonym, of course, not my real name. Anonymity is a good thing in this limbo state. Maybe if I wrote it under a woman's name, it would generate more sympathy, sell more copies. An unusual name too, something catchy."

"What would you call your book?"

"I'll need to think about that. Perhaps 'Stiffed out on life', or how about, 'Pesticide Purgatory'." Eric's mind ticked. "I know – I've got it. I'm going to become a writer and my story will be called, Zombie Reflux."

Part 2: Strange and hallucinatory stories of the mind

The White Kaleidoscope

I was fifteen years old when I was first struck with the desire to eat church candles. The notion swept over me as I slaved away at the till in the department store where I worked every Saturday for a paltry £1.50 an hour.

When I say church candles, I'm talking about a very specific breed. The big, thick, creamy, delicious kind that look like squat marzipan tree trunks. I'm not pregnant, nor deranged; at least, I wasn't the last time I psychoanalysed myself. I've always craved unusual objects. In fact, now that I think of it, my adventuresome palate has landed me in trouble once or twice in the past. Once, being when I masticated the yummy looking psychedelic balls of wool in the dusty classroom cupboard in my nursery school. Twice, being when I chewed my mum's favourite pair of red leather stilettos. In hindsight, it's a bit strange that my pleasant, straight-laced obey-all-the-rules mother had such incriminating shoes hidden in a brown paper bag in the cupboard in the first place.

But we're straying from the point. And I do have a point, believe me. What is it about society that preconditions people to think that only certain items may be deemed worthy enough to be slobbered over? Just think how wide the limited range of foodstuffs would become if we only thought them worthy enough to fill our mouths with? It's like Neanderthals. How can people possibly have a say about them, when they haven't met any? You might think I'm being a tad unfair. Of course, we don't all have time machines that we can just dive into at any given opportunity. But I don't believe in the words 'an educated guess'. What rubbish! How can you claim to understand the wider picture when you don't gather all the data to make a fair judgement? It's like saying that you understand white when you don't even know the primary colours that make it up. Red, yellow and blue, for that matter. That one I learned from my beat-up old encyclopedia. Learned about Neanderthals in there too. Just before I partially digested the book.

I hope you don't mind listening, because I don't mind sitting here and letting the stream of consciousness take over me. Let's get back to candles. I'll tell you how this 'fetish' of mine started. There used to be a young married couple who lived several doors down from my parents' house. They didn't have any kids, so they bought two cats and fussed over them as though they were children. I remember how I used to love those cats. The feel of their soft fur and delicate bodies was soothing. I loved running my greasy little hands over them.

But I made the sorry mistake of trying to feed some salami to the neighbours' cats one day and it didn't go down well. Not my fault, I was only nine. Not old enough to know that they were on a special diet. The man, well, he was too placid anyway and said nothing about the matter. The woman, she got herself into a right old rage, that pug face of hers turned purple as she scolded me. From that day on, I didn't bother with those cats, nor with the couple.

One day, my friend and I were out making candles in her back garden with a new candle making kit she had been given for her birthday, when one of those pesky cats came walking across the back fence. I tell you, an anger swept over me like it never had before and I lobbed a deformed candle through the air at the cat, knocking it off the fence. Well, they say cats have got nine lives, but I'm not so sure. Judging by the racket coming from the other side of the fence where the guard dog lived, I'd say that cat spent all nine in one.

I felt guilty for many years, especially when many a chewed slipper or half eaten tennis ball was hurled over the fence by exasperated guard-dog owners in the succeeding months. The candle lay at the bottom of the garden behind the shed until, consumed with guilt, I snatched it up, wiped it off and ate it whole.

Well, that started the ball rolling. I discovered I have a taste for wax and, as a means of appeasing my guilt, I began my crusade of eating candles. The guilt only subsided after I had a nightmare about those cats. I dreamt that the pair of them were wearing tasselled hats, you know, like the ones graduates wear? And they were sitting on a window ledge, ordering me to eat candles. And I did. I ate and I ate, 'til I was sick. The cats' voices were eerie, haunting. I can still remember, clear as day. The guilt subsided a bit after that. But the craving for candles didn't. The opposite in fact. It progressed and developed into a love for fancier types by the time I was in my teens.

I guess what I learned is that we shouldn't pretend to understand everything, nor should we discriminate against something without having all the knowledge to understand it. I'm not sure if that's possible in only one lifetime. It's like that white I mentioned before.

If you look closer at that white, if you train your eyes for even a moment, you can see the red in the spectrum. Maybe the red is guilt. Is it possible for guilt to extend back into a past lifetime? Sometimes I wonder, especially since I was born with the desire to 'swallow' my guilty passions.

And what of the blue? I say it represents the cyclical wheel of reincarnation. We all carry our foibles into another lifetime. Can you iron out your eccentricities in this life? Hell, I can't!

Then yellow. I think this is the big one. The higher power overseeing us all. Binding it all together. The omnipotent force that interlocks all things. Or am I talking a bunch of Buddhist balderdash?

You decide for yourself. I won't impose it upon you; I won't force it down your throat. But think of the white. Just imagine the kaleidoscope. Like looking through a single lens.

As for me? Well, my story ends with the white alright. My desire to eat candles was quashed by none other than a cat. The poor little critter came across one of my fallen 'comfort' candles and started yakking on it. Oh the pain! The ironic misery! Only the trauma brought on by poetic justice could have halted my cravings. Croaked it there and then. And not only the cat.

Coco and the Black Box

The black dog crouched in the corner of the kitchen. Its teeth were bared and a low, steady growl rumbled from its throat as it fixed its eyes on Mandy. Any minute now the animal would spring and devour her. Mandy's shaking hand gripped the phone. The dialling tone sounded in her ear.

"Pick up, Deanna, please pick up," she whispered.

Deanna's voice cut across the tone. "Hello?"

"Oh thank God - it's Coco. I don't know what to do."

"Not again Mandy. I've told you, you have to get rid of this thing for once and for all."

"Please. I don't know what to do. This devil dog is gonna kill me."

"Because you let it. If it eats you up, it's your own fault. Kick this beast to the curb - put it to rest for your own good, I'm telling you."

"It's not that easy."

"You let it take over your life. Look, I've given you my advice, take it or leave it."

The call ended. Mandy listened to the dead tone. And then, in a flash of black, Coco pounced.

***

Mandy awoke and realised she was lying on the kitchen floor in a pool of her own blood. There was no sign of the dog. She sat up and felt her head throb where it had hit the tiles. Deanna was no help; all she did was chastise her. That wasn't a friend. She had no friends. She had no one. No one except the black dog.

Coco. Why did she even give it a name in the first place? It wasn't a pet. It certainly wasn't anything cute that she wanted to keep. It was a monster, a harmful presence in her life. Deanna was right about one thing; she needed to rid herself of it before it consumed her.

She heard the thing snarling. It was in the hallway. She pulled herself to her feet and stood on her shaky legs. She felt weak. When had she last eaten? Locked away in her flat day after day with only the devil dog in her life tearing everything up, she'd been too preoccupied to worry about trivial things like food and drink. Even sleep had taken its place in her life as a limbo world between life and death; one crazy sleeping-pill induced haze.

A shadow in the corner of her eye told her the beast was lurking. She turned as it came into full view. In one leap, it traversed the gap between hallway and kitchen. In one movement, Mandy rolled clear of its path. The thing hit the wall with a crunch. It fell onto the ground and lay still. Mandy held her breath as she watched. Hopefully it had killed itself.

She ventured a toe to touch the beast. A wet, squelching sound met her ear. Coco's hind quarter stirred; from underneath, a tiny, black puppy emerged. It was a miniature replica of its mother, wriggling out from under the devil dog itself. The beast had given birth to its satanic spawn.

Mandy groaned and massaged her head. Not now. Not this of all things. Not when nobody gave a shit enough to help her.

The pup ran around in circles. It butted Coco's limp side, butted Mandy's foot and raced at the wall.

With a crack, the pup fell back. Now there were two. Mandy rubbed her eyes and willed them to focus. The pup had split in two as it fell to the floor.

The two pups ran around in identical circles of opposite direction. Mandy looked at Coco. The black dog lay on its side, its belly heaving up and down. The thing had a pulse. The thing was alive. It fixed an eye on Mandy and a soft snarl escaped its beastly throat.

"No one cares if I'm alive or dead," said Mandy to the dog. "Mum doesn't even call anymore, no one emails anymore. If you ate me up and I lay here stinking, I wonder how long it would take for people to find me. No one even gives a fuck enough to report me missing."

A sour smell met her nose. Mandy looked down and saw another pup squirming at her feet. The damn dogs were multiplying and there was little she could do to stop it. She wanted to stamp them all out, but that required energy.

"Fuck it. Fuck it all. I hate my life. I hate everything."

She licked her chapped lips. Let the dogs multiply. They could eat her, or eat each other for all she cared.

Two puppies collided. Four fell apart. Like bacteria feeding on a rotting corpse the dogs were spreading. Like fission in a nuclear bomb, they would multiply and destroy everything. A ticking time bomb.

Mandy popped a couple of pills from a blister pack on the kitchen counter and swallowed them to help her throbbing head. She counted nine puppies now rampaging about on the floor. A tenth lay still, near Coco. Looking closer, Mandy noticed that it was dead. As she watched, the black bitch ate her own spawn. A prickle of excitement gripped Mandy.

The momentary happiness gave Mandy a new impulse that she acted on, just to see what would happen; she kicked one of the pups. It flew through the air and landed motionless, but didn't multiply. Three of the other pups fell upon it and ate it. The tiny beasties became frenzied, and she watched them run from the room. Throughout it all, Coco lay, relatively sedate.

"Fuck all the puppies. Fuck all my so called friends. Fuck everyone," she said, feeling anger for the first time in weeks.

Mandy opened the front door and felt the fresh breeze on her face. A grey day. She sighed. Things were never easy for her, but she had to try. She had to take it one step at a time.

One of the puppies bumped against her ankle. She looked down and saw it run into the garden. Her eyes followed it through the grass, before a bird swooped down and attacked it. Mandy watched with mild interest as bird and beast fought. Another puppy down; only eight to go. And the worst of them. The devil dog itself.

"Still, it's all my fault," said Mandy into the breeze. "I gave it a name, and that's how I gave it power. It'll keep growing unless I stop it."

She left the door open to fill the flat with fresh air, and went into her living room. A bar of chocolate lay on the table, half-eaten. Mandy pulled it from the wrapper and ate it in one mouthful. She savoured the taste; her first meal in over twenty-four hours.

Another pup lay dead beneath the glass table. Mandy closed her eyes, the bitter cocoa pleasurable on her tongue. That was her power. She knew now how to do it. She would take the power back for herself.

"I don't need anyone. It's better to have nobody in my life than people who would rather antagonise me."

She looked out the window. The dead carcass of a pup hung in the branches of her hedge, where it had tried to escape. For every part of her life that she reclaimed, a part of her old life died.

Change.

The flat was silent now. One by one, all the pups had died. Another part of her flat had been silenced too, and Mandy knew she had to investigate. She looked in the kitchen, but there was no sign of the black dog.

Coco had gone.

Mandy remembered the front door. Had Coco escaped? Had the beast left for good? If it was true;

that the devil dog had gone, maybe she would be able to start getting her life back together. Maybe she would be able to make new friends. Maybe she could even be sociable once again.

"But I'm scared," said Mandy. "How can I get rid of this fear, this desperation."

Then she saw it; Coco was lying on the roadside. The animal was flat and lifeless, as though it had been run over by a car. With its death, Mandy felt the power return. She had control again, not some black dog in her life. She would start fresh.

A thought niggled at her mind. Mandy shut the front door in case Coco wasn't really dead. If the black dog came back, it would grip her. It would take hold of her and eat her up properly.

A tiny whine made Mandy jump. A puppy sat at her feet. She hadn't killed them all; she had missed one. Instinctively, she stooped and picked it up. The thing looked so tiny and pathetic. How could any of the little monsters ever have controlled her life? Yet she knew the answer; that if she didn't keep it under control, one day it would grow and become another devil dog like Coco.

"What am I to do with you?" she said to the pup. "I can't let you reign free all the time. After all I'm not the only person who has one. Winston Churchill only let his loose at certain times. I've got to do the same with you."

She walked upstairs with the pup held in a tight grip so that it wouldn't escape. In her bedroom was a black jewellery box, given to her as a birthday gift. She had never found a need for it until now, but with its lockable lid, it was the perfect place.

Mandy placed the dog inside. It fit snugly, and looked up at her with its large black-dog eyes. How fitting; a black box for a black dog. A stab of fear overcame her. She would have to make sure the dog didn't get any bigger or it would burst out of its compartment. But for now, it was safe. She closed the lid, muffling a low growl from the animal inside. Mandy smiled and turned the key. It was a day for a new adventure.

Seven Pets for Seven Years

Margarine is the name of my rabbit. I named him Margarine because margarine spreads easier than butter; without the clumps. I hope that my rabbit Margarine will spread just as nicely on toast as the real thing when I make him into a yummy pâté.

Hey now, don't get me wrong! Let me explain myself before you dismiss me as a callous old codger like some twisted farts nowadays can be. Margarine is on his last legs, and I think it's a waste to put such a grand old Flemish giant into the soil when I could cook him up in my copper pot.

It's a shame to bury anything really, never mind a juicy pet. The last time I buried something, it didn't do me any good. After I broke my mirror, I washed the pieces in a south-flowing river and buried them in a forest at the word of a friend, who gave the advice so I wouldn't get seven years of bad luck. Looking back, I might have been better off not being such a superstitious idiot in the first place.

Okay, so you've caught me out. I'm an old cynic. I'll tell you why I've come to be a miserable, pet-eating wretch. Incidentally, it started on the day I broke my mirror.

I was looking into the damn thing while I shaved when it fell off the wall and cracked on the bathroom tiles. I hadn't even touched it, not laid even a single finger on it. If you ask me, the incompetent workman who glued it on the wall, instead of mounting it with nails should have suffered the fate to come for me.

But life ain't fair, right?

So, one at a time, things went tits up after that. My company started making cutbacks and that included my job. My fiancée ran off with some eighteen year old college boy who apparently did some modelling for Christian Dior. La de bloody dah. She was a floozy anyway. And then my house got burgled. They even took half a bottle of opened wine and 50p off my kitchen table. Bastards.

I decided that day that if I'm fated to seven years of bad luck, then I may as well live a life of no guilt to make up for it. I started blaring my TV as loud as I wanted, especially while watching my favourite westerns to give the added sound effects of gunshots and horses. I made a habit of stealing my food staples from the supermarket. Bread, milk and bog roll for free turns pennies into pounds.

And then Butter. Butter was my first pet after my new, cursed lifestyle. He was a Yorkie and didn't taste that good. Too sinewy from catching all those rats. I vowed to get a tastier companion, which is why I bought Margarine from a private seller online.

Since I have nearly four more years of bad luck to go, I'll keep making my own rules for my fate. For every cursed year, I will devour a pet to take back a little of what the world owes me. They'll be well fed all year with plenty of locally stolen delights, so rest assured they'll go out happy like a Christmas turkey. If curses can be instilled, but not reversed, then that to me is a universal imbalance. I will set the balance right for myself by governing my life with my own laws. Seven pets for seven years, I say. Superstitions won't have the better of me, even if life will try.

Arachnid of Life

Life is complex. I sometimes think of it as a spider-web – of how the interconnecting silk is like one problem leading into another. But in such a network, what is the best way to break free of these restraints?

Flexibility. Adaptability.

I consider myself a student of life. Not a student like the one in the story I'm about to tell you, but someone who is flexible, like the legs of a spider working its web.

How easily a student can fall prey to a bigger predator in the pathways that life creates.

I'd like to tell you about an eight year old boy. A small, mousy-haired boy, staring across a table at his support worker. The wooden table top was strewn with the torn remains of a white envelope and its shredded contents.

In the centre of the table stood a leafy bromeliad and I sat behind it, watching adult and child on either side. As I listened to their chat, I watched a minute spider on the bromeliad. And so the web began.

"There was too much mail in the letterbox."

"And so you thought you would lessen it?"

The spider's leg spun, working a web of perfect symmetry.

"It was all stuck–"

The spider stopped. I held my finger over the leaf. What if I wrecked the immaculate web? Would the spider rebuild?

I brought my hand down and perfection died. But silk would linger for an eternity in my mind.

"I ripped it up," said the student.

"But you apologised. So, let's put the incident behind us and learn from it," said the teacher.

"Make a copy."

"I can't. What's done is done."

"I want you to make a copy."

"It's too late. But now you know for next time – don't rip up things that aren't yours. You have to respect other people's property. Nobody goes into your room and rips up your beany babies, do they?"

"No."

"Well then, you should show the same respect to them."

The spider had gone, leaving behind tattered silk.

Sickness rose; what gave me the right to break its web? Who was I to invade its privacy, destroy its property? The spider had spun its web and I had become its prey.

Yet I wouldn't be like the boy. He had listened and not heard, the words floating free, with no trap to keep them.

I was shrinking. Small now. Minute. I lay in the centre of the spider's web and it loomed before me, gigantic.

I couldn't move. I was stuck.

Would I die? No. The spider moved around me. I felt my body sink into a well at the centre, under its own weight. The weight of guilt. I wished the beast would consume me.

The web broke, leaving tattered remains and I fell through. Yet I wasn't dead. Instead of killing me, the spider fell towards me on its silken rope and caught me with its front legs.

Life is complex.

The arachnid had given me new life. Its web had been broken, but it was making a fresh start. And I could see the truth. For every setback in the path, I would learn to keep going. For every day, I would keep spinning a new thread.

Fear of the Mould

Fear of the mould is the inane fear of fear itself.
Fear is the smell of decay; a worry that the
mould will catch up with you, that the spores of
the old place will infest the new. Is everything polluted?
Contaminated?

Fear is that spreading sewage behind the walls: the
brown speckled patterns on whitewashed walls. Only
this time, it's in you. And even though you cleaned the
four walls that boxed you in, even though you
scrubbed them with a sponge and bleach, you fear the
rot has already set in and will come back. You've
moved on, run away - but you haven't escaped. You

can smell the mould in your clothes and hair. Yet it doesn't taint those around you: only you.

The four walls of the new courtyard should give you safety, but they don't. You're alone with the fear. It has desensitised you. All the smells in this new place are unfamiliar and so you feel detached, alien. You cook, you spray air freshener, but you can't shake off the old, damp smell of lingering, festering evil underlying it all.

You walk the busy streets of the big city. Though the people pass you by, you feel a fleeting desperation; you want to shake off this rot but you can't. Talking about it to someone gives you temporary relief, but still the fear crawls. It seeps under the surface, the same as in the old place. The old place is empty now, but you had to go back to clean it through contractual obligations; even now it lures you back. As you cleaned, you saw the blackness on the sponge; the fetid stains on your hands. You worked without any clothes on so it wouldn't taint them, but it didn't help. You wore a surgical mask filled with scented oil, but still the death-spores stung your eyes.

The mould creeps into your mind at night and leaves you in a cold sweat. It trickles into your guts, making them squirm, filling you with the gas of pain. You know what the mould means - so many bad events happened in that place, so many evil memories that slipped behind the dreaded walls, weaved themselves into the fabric of the building.

The escape doesn't feel real for you. You feel that the new place has the air of holiday about it; artificial, unreal. The fear is that it is all a dream, that the new life will be whipped from under you and you will be back at the old place. Back in the rot. Unable to leave the stench.

The rot is a fear of the monster within you; a conjugation of the evil that they inflicted upon you, and your own powers of perpetuation. The mould threatens to rear its ugly head inside your own soul, to eat you from the inside out.

But you are on a high floor now in the new place. These four walls of the courtyard can set you free. By facing the evil, instead of denying it and letting it fester, you have shed the rot. The clothes no longer smell. The air smells of the home you have made. You have left the monsters behind – you will not become the next generation of rot. You will not continue the cycle of fear. You can feel the wings on your back. The window opens towards an endless sky. Your wings will take you to a new beginning.

House of Cards

At night I'm an angel. I unfold my seraphic wings and take flight from the roof of St. George's Wharf. I glide free towards distant mountains, across blue skies, feeling the cool air ripple through my feathers. But then I start to descend; an invisible weight pulls me down. I always wake up at that point. If only life could be so easy. Maybe for someone else, though not for me.

***

I stood by the Thames, looking towards Vauxhall Bridge. It was a brisk day, though mild for winter. As I read the tourist sign, I visualised the Bronze Age bridge that once stretched out into the river, 4000 years before the present-day bridge. The Thames would have been much wider then, and marshy. Maybe the ash and birch bridge connected the land to an island. It could even have been a sacrificial place for offerings to Pagan gods. If it were here, now, I would have offered myself to the river. I couldn't help but feel that winter was closing in on my life, my days becoming shorter and bleaker.

***

It's the same dream again; I'm an angel. Only, this time, there are changes. I'm standing in front of the pharmacy at St. George's Wharf, and I unfold my angel wings. I fly upwards but a small, white package in my arms weighs me down. I want to fly into the freedom of the crisp air. But I get pulled back to earth.

***

It was day again, and the stark greyness of reality loomed over me. I looked down at the blister pack in my hand. Citalopram. My doctor told me to take the antidepressants in the evening, as apparently for most people, the sadness takes over at night. But the despair that I feel eats at me every day. My sole means of help are my daily walks on the pebbly strand in front of St. George's Wharf. I call it, my beach.

I walked over to the rotten stump that in its glory days would have made up one post of many in the ancient bridge traversing the Thames. I felt that there was also mould clinging to me, as there was on the decayed wood. I wanted to escape the gloom, but I could see no light at the end of the tunnel.

"Are you alright there?" asked a man's voice, behind me.

I turned. He was middle-aged, wearing a storm-proof jacket, and holding a metal detector in one hand.

"You looked so sad, I thought I'd ask what's the matter," he said.

"I'm fine," I said. "I come down here to think sometimes."

"Better watch your musings don't get you carried away - the tide's coming in."

I looked out at the murky water. I'd sometimes wondered what it would be like to drown. To fall off Vauxhall Bridge into a strong current. Neither romantic, nor mystical, I would imagine. Centuries of anaerobic filth was enough to deter me from that line of morbid curiosity.

"If I get swept off, then it can't be helped. I wouldn't be missing much," I said in an undertone. My words were whipped away on the breeze. The man's eyes searched my face for a moment, before he turned and walked up the steps. I looked once more out at the Thames and felt a dark curtain curl around me.

***

I'm inside a luxury apartment at St. George's Wharf, but within all the modern glass and metal fixings, I'm trapped. There's been a terrorist alert from MI6 across the way. I can see men in balaclavas running amok outside. There's carnage everywhere - bodies littering the streets, great fires. Then I see it. It's a great dragon, cold and metallic. It's crushing buildings in its path, moving towards where I am. But I'm stuck. There is no door. The only thing I can do is hide – roll myself in the curtain, hold my breath and pretend I don't exist…

***

I went down to my place of solace again, my beach. This time I stood on the strand in front of MI6. In the legend, St. George fought a dragon – he was a great hero, the defender of England. What was I fighting? Was the dragon of my dreams someone in my life? Or my life itself? Perhaps it was a metaphysical thing; the blackness that was consuming me.

"Good day to you again," said the same man from the day before.

"Hello," I said. I stooped and picked up a fragment of shell. Then, with a sigh, I threw it out to the waves.

"That bad, eh?" he said.

"What do you mean?" I asked.

"The storm."

"I don't know what you're talking about," I answered, avoiding his gaze.

"It's a warzone going on in there, isn't it?"

I looked him right in the eye. How could he possibly have known about my dream?

Of course, he couldn't have. I was being melodramatic. I turned my eyes back to the pebbly shore. It must've been obvious on my face. Was I really that much of an emotional wreck that my expressions displayed the inner turmoil openly?

"I have a few things on my mind, that's all," I said.

"I know. I've been there myself. You want to throw yourself to the tide, but you can't. You think of all the people you would hurt - you don't want to cause them pain."

I looked at the water and tears pooled in my eyes.

"It's a good thing to worry about the people you love," said the man. "It means you're far from danger. You won't do it."

"Who says I wouldn't? I'm not a coward," I said.

"I didn't say you were. But you *are* a house of cards. If one is pulled from the bottom, the whole thing will come toppling down."

I wiped away my tears and looked up. "I'm not that fragile. I've just had enough of life. There's nothing much to live for. Nothing seems to go my way. So what's the point?"

"You know what your problem is? Your way of thinking. You get into this negative mindset and it sets off a chain reaction that pulls you further and further down. If you want to tie a boulder to your leg and throw yourself to the bottom of the Thames, go ahead. Feel sorry for yourself. But on the other hand, you could be a bit more resourceful. Every situation requires an appropriate response. And when times change, the response changes. That's how people have survived for thousands of years. They adapt. Don't be the boulder, be the water. It can freeze, boil, flow, crash - break all the rocks on this beach."

I absorbed the man's words, but I had no answer. All throughout my life, I had wanted to be the angel of my dreams; saving people, saving myself. Now it was my turn to be saved. I imagined the prehistoric bridge again. Ash and birch were flexible types of wood. They could bend, withstand restraint. I needed to be flexible and adaptable too. I needed to cross my own bridge over the stormy waters, not fall in.

***

I'm an angel again. The war is over. I'm safe. I'm here to heal the ones I love, not hurt them. Most of all, I have to heal myself. I fly free from my rooftop abode, and this time I don't come down.

***

I went back to my beach, and I knew it would be the last time. I had the Citalopram in my hand. I didn't need it anymore. As I brought my hand up and threw the blister pack into the waves, I thought of the man who had helped me to save myself.

I turned and walked along the pebbly shore, this time alone. Pieces of sea-glass littered the strand. They were wave-worn, rounded; adapted to a life drifting free to wherever the tide could carry them. So too could I.

I continued along the shore towards the end. The stretch of beach below my feet narrowed, the pebbles becoming more scattered, the pieces of shell fewer. The strand tapered into a triangular point where the water met the land. I let the waves wash over my feet.

The Existence of Things Inside Wall Spaces

What exists in the gap between bricks? The gap where the mortar has crumbled away as aggregates of time. I have to know. I have to know, like the Canadian geese have to know the way back from Ireland in the spring. I have to look.

I'm looking. Not into the interior of a house, but into a small hole. Inside the hole is a miniature spinning wheel, not more than an inch big, and beside it, a pair of silk mittens, like mocha-coloured oven gloves. They seem to have a ferrous tinge from the orange brick. As my eyes scour the space, I see mocha-coloured silk threads zigzagging their way from upper to lower facets of brick.

Where I'm looking, a chunk of plaster is missing from the wall, as if someone spent a good deal of time carefully peeling it away from the brick. I'm guessing it was a bored child. A stuffy child, probably a spoiled kid with a pudgy face, and an ill demeanour.

Now, I too am peeling the plaster. The white flakes coming away in my hand are not more than half a centimetre thick and are leaving a powdery white residue on my palm and under my nails. Beneath, the brick is tangerine orange.

And what is this I see? A psychedelic greenish-blue blob about two inches long. I extend my finger to investigate.

It moves! A caterpillar, plump and feisty, living under the plaster. How on earth did such a juicy fellow fit under that packed space?

The caterpillar makes its way along the crease of the brick towards the gap. Oh no. No you don't! No quick escape for you when I'm in such an inquisitive mood!

The thing wriggles and, afraid it might drop, I encourage it onto my hand. My, oh my, what sticky legs it has, I needn't have worried in the first place.

Did this little beastie spin the silk threads? This squishy critter knitting tiny oven gloves at the minute spinning wheel, and who knows what other things that fill the space between bricks? Oh the things Canadian geese would only know if they looked below on their journey!

I'm glad I wasn't inclined to transcend that gap. How easy it could have been to not look inside. When you're enroute from A to B, a straight line is the quickest way. Not to mention the least complicated. I'd like to say it was coincidence, but I'm not so sure. If you bother to look inside a world, there's another smaller world tucked inside it.

Blue-green caterpillars only happen on a crescent moon. When the sky is a backwash of clouds swept away by a tide of silken thread. And sometimes if you focus too much on the path to the moon, you might miss all the heavenly glory.

Glen Abbot and the Green Man

Glen Abbot waited at the traffic lights as cars, buses and vans streamed by in the hazy sunlight. He looked at his watch and sighed.

"Takes forever, doesn't it?" said a man's voice next to him.

Glen turned and set eyes on his neighbour, then yelped with fright and fell back against the traffic-light post. The green man from the signal stood next to him; all six-foot of it from shoeless feet to smooth, bald head.

Glen wiped his sweaty brow. Either the summer heat was getting to him or he'd hit his head harder than he had thought at the weekend.

No; there had to be a rational explanation first. It had to be a man wearing a costume of sorts.

"Are you going to a party?" Glen asked.

The green man shook his head. "Why do you ask?"

"Strange costume. I mean, how do you breathe in that thing anyway, with no eye, nose or mouth holes? Is it some sort of new material?"

"Costume? What material? I'm not sure what you mean, but I am what I am."

Glen looked up at the traffic signal. The red man had been showing for a long time, the screen above black and empty. He looked across at his companion and comprehension dawned. He was having hallucinations caused by his severe concussion - that had to be it.

"What a lazy great sod he is," said the green man, jerking his round dome of a head towards the red man. "That'll teach him - he can pull his weight for a change!"

"This is nuts," said Glen. "Am I the only one who can see you?"

"Oh please!" said the green man. "I'd like to hope not, considering what I'm about to do. Took me ages to climb down from that post, and I wouldn't do it if I was some kind of non-entity, like yourself."

"Me?" said Glen, raising his eyebrow. "Why, what makes you so important?"

"Well, I do more with my life than sit at home, for a start. Drinking whiskey and rotting your brain watching telly all day - it's no wonder you see me better than the others. What's your name anyway?"

Glen clenched his teeth. This hallucination was going a bit far; his imagination had never been so rude to him before. "Glen Abbot," he answered with a frown.

"That's a nice name. Sounds almost like a Scotch," said the green man.

"That's why I picked it. Glen Abbot Tomlinson."

"Of course - to wash down all the beer you drink," said the green man. "I don't have a name. Most people call me, 'about time', or 'let's go'."

Glen smirked. "How are we supposed to cross the road if you're down here, then? Isn't that the whole point of you - to make it safe for people to cross?"

The green man shrugged. "Yeah, pretty mundane life, eh? But not anymore. I reckon we make a dash for it."

"Well, you'd know best. You're the green man. Lead the way."

Glen followed him into the traffic, weaving between the cars. Nobody seemed to even give a second glance to the green man as they passed. It had to be the strangest hallucination he'd ever had.

"What's this thing you're off to do that's so important anyway?" asked Glen.

"It sounds a bit convoluted," said the green man.

Glen grinned. "You're a green man? What could it possibly be apart from flashing at a few people?"

"To tell you the truth, when you're hanging up there waiting for your turn to shine for twenty-four hours a day, three hundred and sixty-five days a year, you start to see the world in a new light. There are certain things that bother me about society."

"Like what?" said Glen.

"Two words," said the green man. "Chewing gum. The damn kids! They stick it all over my post. One time this nasty, fat little brat even climbed up and stuck a chewing gum hat right on my head!"

"Yeah, but what can you do about it? Society won't change."

"That's what you think. There's a green party campaign today on today down at Parliament Square, so I'm going along - who better than me to support a good cause for our planet? I'm a pretty good mascot being the colour that I am, don't you think?"

Glen Abbot nodded. "Yeah, I suppose you are."

"And that's just the first step. I have bigger plans too. I want a law passed in this country like they have in Singapore - jail for people who litter the place with chewing gum. Oh yes, I'm going to do it. I'm going to clean up this town. I'm going to start my own party - I'll be a politician!"

"Sounds like a better idea than what I was going to do with *my* afternoon," said Glen. "I was going to order a takeaway and watch the match."

Definitely, it was the best delusion he'd ever had. How many dreams turned into reality? And even odder, how many strange entities were motivated by a good cause? So long as it was going to last, Glen made up his mind.

"If you want, I'll be your canvasser," he said.

The green man stuck out his stump to Glen and they exchanged a handshake of sorts.

"Yes, Glen Abbot who sounds like a whiskey, that sounds like a perfect idea to me. Together we'll make things right. With your humanity and my brilliance, we'll be sure to get what I want."

Glen smiled too. It would most likely all be over tomorrow, but for now, he was enjoying himself. It was certainly a more interesting use of his time than getting hammered and falling down the stairs. His steps fell in sync with the neon-green legs of his new leader as they walked towards the green demonstration and a brighter future.

The Art of Something Out of Nothing

The wheeled trunk was as long as the traveller was tall. The weight of the trunk didn't matter since the traveller had the girth of a tree. This country was warmer than the last and windier too. The humidity curled the sinusoidal waves of the traveller's hair into tight coils. Sin. Sin-u-soidal. Soil. New soil. The past could be buried; sin could be buried in soil. Like everything else about the traveller, their hair had no fixed state, just as they had no fixed state and at any moment, the hydrogen bonds of their hair could break and reform, leaving their hair in lank strands. The traveller was a lank strand in a new country, a new place, on new soil. A tourist.

The tourist could walk forever if they had to in their travel-worn shoes. The travel-worn shoes had morphed over time into a comfortable smart-casual mould of the tourist's feet. But they walked on their toes. Their calves were tight from always walking on the balls of their feet.

This new place had an unknown smell. An unexamined scent of victory. Though still, they walked tip-toe, tip-toe, tip-toe, always on edge, always ready.

Escape was undeniable, invisibility inevitable.

The trunk didn't contain anything that couldn't be brought without bringing down the hammer of incrimination. Negative words, negative thoughts, negating the needless nacre of the trunk. The trunk was clunky. It was a clunky trunk. The trunk went clunk. The thoughts were choppy. The thoughts needed to be chopped up. Chopped up and dissipated.

Tip-toe, feeling the breeze, causing a shirt to ripple and flap against a tip-toe-tensed body. The wind passed by. It was a passive wind.

Full circle from touch-down-to-taxi-to-rest-on-stand-to-tip-toe-to transcending the double automatic doors, wheeling the trunk behind. Clunk-clunky it clicked outside onto the tarmac.

The trunk contained anything necessary to remember remnants of a past time in a passive voice.

The traveller looked back over their shoulder, feeling the drag.

And then, the tourist walked forward, towards the sun over a new country, into a fresh life. Breaking the rules.

Don't Feed the Cats

"Didn't you hear me? I said, don't feed the cats!"

Bill turned and looked at his mother. He scratched his nose and extended his arm out the back door, ready to drop the scraps.

"I don't see what's the harm. The poor things will starve if we don't feed them."

"They can go to their owners if they want food. We're not some blasted cat charity service. And put your lip in while you're at it. Hanging there like a wet flannel over a broken towel rail, I dunno. Face tripping you all the time these days–" She shuffled away, shaking her head.

"Oh, alright then," Bill shouted at her retreating back. He closed the back door and stomped over to the bin to get rid of the scraps.

"And you can cut out the sulking while you're at it. A great lump like you? You're not a child anymore."

Bill decided not to retaliate. He knew better than to cross her when she was in one of her moods. Though these days, one of her moods seemed to be every second. Menopause was her excuse. His parents' words met his ear clearly through the bannister as he climbed the stairs, making his upper lip twitch.

"...The trouble is, the neighbours have been complaining to the council about rats. They say it's cos of all the food thrown out for the cats. If you ask me, Bill's the worst culprit behind it all. Feed the blasted cats, feed the birds, feed the fucking hedgehogs."

"...Aw, lay off the lad, he's only trying to do some good. Better than being one of those little thugs who tear up cars and steal bikes."

"...Well, I suppose that's true, still–"

He tiptoed on up to his bedroom. Lying in the cool of his dark room, he felt relaxed. The walls were adorned with posters showing the signs of the Zodiac and, in particular, the new age of Aquarius soon to come, the Babylonian map of the world, a timeline showing human history up until the year 2012, charts depicting the seven chakras of the human body among others. Namely old high school stuff. The room was where he went to meditate. His life needed an occasional rebalancing, and the posters helped him to focus. Though according to the weather forecast, a thunderstorm was on its way. Nothing better than bad weather for calming the mind.

As the dark clouds rolled in, Bill grabbed his umbrella. Thankfully, nobody was downstairs when he entered the living room. The TV was on loud enough to wake the dead and he caught a glimpse of an audience clapping as a host cracked a joke. Useless shit. What good was it for anyway? Nothing more than another means of keeping the population subdued. If they were all hypnotised, they were easy to manipulate. His Zeitgeist DVD warned of such brainwashing. Individuality was a key component of transcending to a higher spiritual dimension in the age of Aquarius soon to come.

Bill needed his mind clear. His psychic guide, Cindy, told him that he needed to be more grounded in reality. His thoughts were all too often in transcendental ethers, which wasn't good for him since his chakras were already blocked by strong interference from past lives. He was trying his best. The fifth dimension was the last place where evil could reside, she told him, and he was working hard to purge his life of all previous residue. It didn't help that he had been high up in the Freemasons once before and had laundered money for the secret world bank in Switzerland, and a dark prince another time who had sold his own people as slaves to the enemy after consulting an obsidian mirror. In another past life, he had tried to rectify the damage as a Colonel in the S.S, who had tried to help Jews escape from Warsaw, but had been captured and didn't finish the good deed. In all his past lives, people had suffered as a result of his power. Now he was working to channel that knowledge for good, not evil. It really was tough living as such a high spiritual being with a raised level of consciousness when he had parents who did their best to demean him and no real money to call his own. Still. He slid a hand into his pocket and felt for the small polythene bag. Rubbing it between his thumb and forefinger to feel the coarseness of the plant fibres inside, he smiled. The Shamans of Stonehenge and Atlantis knew the secrets of the herbs for millennia and had passed them down to only a privileged few. Cindy was in the direct bloodline of the original shamans, and had set him up with a secret supplier, her astral twin, Mahgogh.

As he passed into the kitchen, Bill saw fat droplets smash against the window pane outside. He opened the door to the back garden, glad that night had fallen early due to the storm. The rain plopped onto his umbrella. One or two rebellious raindrops splattered his cheeks. He fumbled in his pocket, his fingers catching a few strands of dried plant. Onto his tongue. Bitter. He closed his eyes against the onslaught from the heavens and savoured the taste for a brief moment. Then he planted himself on a sawn-off tree-stump, the metal rod of the umbrella wedged in his armpit. He crossed his legs into a half-lotus and relaxed.

Lightning flashed above. The sky shone pink in the glare. Bill let his eyes glaze over as he stared at a point several cubits straight ahead. The rain drummed a rhythm on the plastic of the umbrella. He felt as hypnotised as the people on TV had been. What was life anyway, if not one big gameshow?

Nothing ahead. Darkness and, beyond it, the fence at the bottom of the garden. A few shrubs. Bill's eyes gazed upwards at the purplish clouds. The raindrops were silvery in the light from a nearby lamppost.

It came at first as a fragmented image. An outline of a cheek. A temple. Chiselled. Indeterminable if it was male or female. An eye. Almond shaped, high and sloping downwards towards a tear duct closely set to a well sculpted nose. The bridge of the nose tapered, finishing in a pinched stub. Then he saw hair, long and curling. It was reflected golden in the flashes from the storm. The long locks framed a heart-shaped face that was set by two pointed ears like triangles on top of the head. A cat-like being. More beautiful and graceful than man. An Arcturian.

Bill gasped and the vision was gone.

It had been floating like a dream, suspended in the air in front of him. In its absence, the darkness seemed more intense as if he had been robbed of a precious possession and left with an empty space. But no, there was more. There was movement.

He squinted into the gloom. Yes, somebody was there. The snapping of a twig announced the presence of another being in the vicinity. Bill felt his body tense.

"Who's out there?"

No reply. Silence.

And then a breath, heavy on the moist air.

"Shit!" said a woman in a voice close to a hiss.

"Mum?" said Bill.

Then he saw her, stumbling between bushes a few feet away. Even behind the foliage, he could see that she was semi-dressed. Her short denim skirt was riding high on her thighs and she was wearing only her bra, carrying her shirt in one hand. Behind her–

Bill fell off his tree stump. He couldn't believe what his eyes were showing him.

His mother was having an affair with an Arcturian being.

"Get the hell back into that house!" his mother yelled. "This is none of your damn business!"

And her fists rained down on him, fiercer than a thunderclap, heavier than a fell smiting from Mjölnir.

***

So, he had finally done it. He had raised his consciousness to a high enough level that it had opened a channel between earth and the distant star, Arcturus. Only ascended spirits on earth were able to communicate with higher beings. Bill let his chest expand as he sucked in a deep breath of air.

Then what about his mother? Not just communicating, but having a full blown affair with one. He exhaled, his shoulders slumping.

Bill made sure to trim the fat off the meat and cut it into bite-sized chunks before placing the pieces tenderly on a saucer. Funnily enough, he had no more complaints from his mother as he fed the cats over the next few days. Nor did they talk to one another. What was he supposed to say to her? So, you're cheating on dad then? By sleeping with an alien from a more enlightened world?

Was it an insult or a compliment? On the one hand, seeing Arcturians meant that he had raised his psychic intuition to a deeper spiritual level. He wouldn't have seen his mother's lover if it wasn't for his higher understanding. It would have looked like she was frolicking all by herself. But, on the other hand those higher beings were a potential cause of great havoc in his earthly life. And whether he liked to admit it or not, he was stuck on earth until he gathered enough knowledge to move beyond his physical body.

"The cats really enjoy this food. Very nutritious for their cat-like ways," said Bill over his shoulder with a knowing smile, as he put the remnants of the Sunday roast outside. His mother fixed him with a warning stare, but said nothing. Bill felt a tremor of pleasure. He loved having the upper hand.

"Or is it rats, mum? Am I attracting rats rather than cats with all my scraps?" Bill dusted off his hands and closed the door. "That has a nice ring to it, don't you think? Rats. Cats. Scraps. I should be a poet. The things poets write about."

He could see her face redden; the calm before the storm.

"That's enough! That's about all I'm gonna take from you!"

Bill widened his eyes in mock protest. "What did I say? Sounds like I've accused you of something. Unless you're admitting to something that I don't know about?"

At that comment, his father looked away from the TV and fixed him with a stare. "What are you getting at, son?"

Bill dropped his grin.

"I think he means he's the rat!" said his mother. "The biggest damn rat of them all. Clear off out of my sight. Go on! You lay-about!"

Bill narrowly missed her hand as he slipped out of the kitchen. Maybe he was taking things too far. If his mother really was having an affair, did he want his father to know about it? If they got divorced, then it would all be on his conscience. And he didn't want anything to interfere with the higher wavelength he was now operating on.

The cats were coming for their food. One was skulking near the fence. Another padded across the wet lawn. Bill watched as the bushes ruffled and then parted. It stood amidst the shaggy mass of branches, master of all cats.

Bipedal like humans, yet no more than five foot tall. Bill's feet propelled him towards it, the saucer dangling in his hand like an extra, deformed limb. It made no attempt to move or run but simply waited for him to come, it's dazzling green eyes fixed on him. Hypnotic.

"Welcome," said Bill, "To the earthly plane."

The Arcturian dipped its head, one ear pointing horizontally to the side.

"You are on the right path to enlightenment, my friend," it beamed into his brain telepathically.

Bill was seized with several confusing messages at once. The urge to strike it, to punch it on the nose overwhelmed him. At the same time, he felt a desire to bow down before it. What a tremendous compliment. To be a master while still in the flesh! Instead, his assembled thoughts manifested themselves in a manner that surprised even him.

"Would you like to come for dinner?" said Bill.

***

"Mum? Where are you? I need to ask if something is okay?"

"What are you yakking on about?" said Bill's dad.

Bill pursed his lips. "I'm not yakking, dad. I'm trying to ask a question. Where is she?"

"I'm coming!" The sound of a toilet flushing grew louder as a door opened and slammed shut. "What the hell is it now?"

"I wanna know if it's okay to have a – a companion over for dinner tomorrow."

"A companion? Speak English for crying out loud! Are you talking about a friend? Cos I can't imagine a useless tub of lard like you having a girlfriend."

Bill rolled his eyes. "Just answer the question, would you? Is it okay or isn't it?"

She pushed past him and lit up a cigarette over the kitchen sink. "I suppose so. Just don't expect anything fancy. We're having bangers and mash. I'm not splashing out to feed some lay-about friend of yours. Twenty-three and still at home on incapacity benefit. I don't know."

Bill watched her shaking her head and left her to mutter to herself over her cigarette. Bangers and mash was perfect. Some good old British culinary delights to introduce the Arcturian to. Cats liked sausages and potatoes, right?

But what would the superior being think of his family's dinner habits? It was customary in their household to eat in front of the TV. Bill usually sat with his plate in his lap and a drink on the coffee table. Maybe a proper family meal would be better.

He started the preparations early the following day. After moving the coffee table to one side, he cleared the trinkets and photos from a family trip to the Isle of Man off the collapsible table and unfolded it in the centre of the room. In one of the kitchen drawers was a mouldy old lace table cloth which he threw over it, and he found plastic place mats from Christmas in another drawer. He switched the TV off and unplugged it to avoid distractions. As Bill was laying out the knives and forks in their correct places, he realised the most important thing he had forgotten to do; he hadn't told the Arcturian what time to arrive.

As his mother bustled by holding plates and pots full of steaming food, Bill made his way to the back door and stood overlooking the garden as he had done the previous night. Nothing. No movement apart from the trees swaying in the breeze.

Muttering a shamanic conjuration, Bill made himself a cup of his special herbal tea for Dutch courage. Now all he needed was bait. A packet of ham would suffice. He ripped it open and shredded the contents, emptying the pieces on the ground. The cats came right away through gaps in the fence. And then he saw it. A disturbance in the bushes at the end of the garden.

"Hello again," said Bill. "You're just in time."

The Arcturian dipped its head in response and moved past Bill into the house. The cat-like being walked so smoothly, it was as if it was gliding.

A sour thought crossed his mind. He had been too excited and preoccupied with the alien coming to tea to think about the potential consequences. He was bringing the enemy, his mother's lover, into the household to enhance the rift between his parents. A sinking feeling overcame him. Too late for regrets now.

As he entered the living room, Bill saw that the Arcturian was already seated. Adjacent to it at the head of the table sat his father with his hands on his lap, staring ahead, his eyes unfocussed.

"Bill?" said his mother from the kitchen. "Where is that damn kid?"

"I'm coming."

"Make use of yourself. Take this pot."

Bill carried the large pot of mash through to the living room, his mother following behind with a dish full of sausages. As he set the pot down, he saw her halt, almost dropping the dish. A lone sausage tumbled to the floor.

"What's going on?" said his mother, her face beetroot. She looked from the Arcturian to Bill. Bill saw her straighten up as she regained her composure. Bill made a beeline for the buttered peas, a narrow escape.

"Eh- nice to meet you," she said, sticking out a hand to the guest. "I'm Claire."

"Juliano," said the Arcturian. "Enlightened."

She took the creature's cat-like paw in her hand, her fingers closing around the splayed toes and shook. Quite the exaggerated gesture. Bill felt heat creep into his face as his mother took her seat opposite his father.

As he sat in the remaining seat facing Juliano, Bill began loading up his plate without speaking. What was going on? Okay, so his mother's odd behaviour was normal, her adultery was being laid on a plate as plain as the sausages. But what of his dad? Wasn't he even in the least bit–

"Dad, you've met Juliano, haven't you?"

"What's that son?" he said, through a mouthful of mash.

Bill tried to read his eyes behind the reflection of his glasses. "Never mind."

"Then why are you wasting time talking? Tuck in."

Silence fell and Bill shifted in his seat. He dug the spoon into the buttered peas and moved the scoop towards his plate, but his hand was shaking too much. Miniature green cannon balls rolled towards Juliano, as if they were magnetized. He reached into his pocket, fumbling inside the plastic bag and caught a few herb fragments with the tips of his fingers. His own special seasoning and a mid-dinner relaxant at the same time.

"Er – so what's it like where you're from Juliano?" said Bill.

"Quite hot, but not uncomfortably so." Juliano took a dainty bite of sausage and chewed with feline grace.

"How long did it take you to get here?"

"It was instantaneous. I'm always around."

Cryptic. Bill watched the being as the peas rolled around his mouth. "Do the cats always come to you?"

"I have a great connection with them. They bond well with me."

The clink of cutlery on crockery filled the air, smacking lips and the occasional grunt. A million questions blossomed in Bill's brain.

"I saw Dave today across the road," said Bill's dad with a thick tongue.

"Was it dead?" said Bill's mother, forking a sausage.

A hesitation followed. "He's not dead, he just got back from holiday."

Another pause. "What are you on about? Wouldn't it be quarantined?"

Bill looked from his father to mother, confused. Juliano kept eating, looking at his plate.

"What are you on about?" said his dad swallowing his food. "I'm talking about Dave."

"Oh, *Dave*! I thought you said *deer*. You shouldn't ruddy-well talk with your mouth full."

His dad rolled his eyes and went back to his food. Silence fell once again.

Bill looked down at the TV plug lying on the floor, the prongs facing upwards. Any old crap show would be better than a lack of conversation. What would Juliano think?

Apparently it agrced. The Arcturian dabbed its mouth on a Christmas napkin and pushed its seat back from the table, standing up.

"Well, thank you for a lovely dinner, but I must be going now."

"What – so soon?" said Bill's mother and Bill stared at her. She caught sight of him and averted her gaze. "We have dessert, is all."

Juliano smiled. "A kind offer, but I feel I've imposed upon you enough as it is." The creature offered a bow to all and padded towards the kitchen. Bill started to see it out, but his mother had rushed ahead closely tailing it. Bill turned to look at his father. The man was chewing with bulging cheeks, oblivious to the whole situation.

Bill plugged the TV in and let the sounds and colours wash over him. How on earth were these people able to see the Arcturian too? He balled his hands into fists.

His mother came back in looking windswept and sat back down, tucking her hair behind an ear. She speared another sausage and started chewing it on the fork.

"What's going on?" said Bill, looking from his dad, to his mum.

"That's what I'd like to know," said his dad. "How long has it been going on, Irene?"

"Irene?" said Bill, his scalp pulling taut. "But mum's name's Claire–"

"Only Irene would cheat," said his father, staring across the table at her. "How long?"

She shrugged. "A few weeks. Maybe a month."

"Am I hearing this right?" said Bill, leaning his elbows on the table. "You're worried about the fact that mum's cheating, and not about who with?"

"Oh, I know who *with* alright. He's a bloke from down the pub."

"The pub? Dad, what are you on about?"

"The Cat in the Sack, that new pub on the corner of–"

"Dad, don't you see? He's not some bloke from the Cat in the Sack, he's an Arcturian," Bill shouted, exasperated.

Dad's lip trembled. "Shakespearean, not Arcturian. He might be a damn decent actor, but he's a dandy nonetheless. Imagine dressing up as a cat. I suppose you put him up to that, Irene, since I wouldn't dress up for you."

"Fine. So, I have a cat fetish, what's the big deal? It's not like you indulge me with any creative play these days. I have to get my kicks somehow. Not to mention that he's one hell of a lover!"

Bill threw his hands up. "Dad, don't you even give a damn that mum's seeing an Arcturian? Don't you know what this means?"

"He's Brazilian actually," said his mother, slouching back in her chair, arms folded.

"Brazilian? Shakespearean? How can you both avoid the point? Just say the word, for crying out loud." Bill ran his hands through his hair. His mouth felt dry. "It's Arcturian!"

Mum turned puce. "Yes, Arthurian. He was playing King Arthur when I saw him on stage and all I know is, he's a ruddy fine Arthurian actor, who's willing to do cat cosplay and – damn it – it's the most fun I've had in years!"

Bill felt a rush of hot blood pumping in his chest. They didn't deserve it, to see Juliano or to talk to him, never mind his mother sleeping with him. How could she possibly be a higher spiritual soul if she was too focused on earthly pleasures?

He felt his frown dissolve. That was it. So simple. It was another challenge of his spirit, another step to climb on the ladder to enlightenment. An image of Juliano appeared before his eyes. The golden cat-fur dissolved into olive skin, the feline eyes changed into dark, sultry Latino ones that had enticed his mum. Bill shook his head to clear the image. Juliano had set up a scenario to test him, by pretending to be human and having an affair with his mother. It was all to see if his soul was strong enough, ready for more. He had to overcome this dilemma of the physical plane in order to placate his consciousness. Bill smiled to himself. He reached into his pocket and extracted a few more strands of his special herbs, which he placed in his mouth. His family saw Juliano as a Brazilian, Arthurian, Shakespearean actor, but he saw to a deeper level of understanding. Swimming before his dilated pupils, he alone saw the truth.

Jim

Jim sashayed up to the bus stop, his shoulder bag swinging in time to his rhythm, his bowler hat tipped to the left. He smoothed his pinstripe jacket with both hands, then wiped his palms on his jeans. He had spotted her. Mid-forties, platinum hair, pencil skirt. Office worker. In one fluid move, he had closed the gap before she even had time to look up from her bus schedule. Then, he slipped an arm around her waist touching the curve of her back and pressed his lips to hers. She made a noise of surprise, then responded with years of pent-up desire.

He peeled her off with a light touch on her shoulder. He had spotted her again: five feet four and black with red weaved through her dark braids. Glasses. No worries. She was walking towards the bus stop, each foot crossing the path of the other. He sidled up and stood in her path, stopping her. He looked down at her and gave his best boyish smile. Then he moved his face to hers. Closer. Closer. Her glasses steamed up and her breathing came: heavy, heavy. She pulled back from him and he could see her melt in his grin. He spun her around and watched her continue on her way, her tempo not so smooth now.

He saw her a third time, leaning against the bus shelter with her eyes closed. Engrossed in her music. Late teens, a few years younger than him. Blue-black hair, dyed. Nose piercing. He swooped over and touched her chin with the tips of two fingers, pushed her face up until her green eyes met his. He saw a slight flush wash over her freckled cheeks. Then his lips met her slightly parted mouth.

The bus came. Jim pulled away and their lips gave a final wet smack. He hopped onto the bus, his trainers making no sound, and left her staggering aboard behind him. He glided down the aisle and took a seat near the back, all eyes looking up as he passed.

Jim.

The bus rumbled on to the next stop. The drone of conversation fell as a man got on, six four and built like an ox, his trapezius muscles sloping from shoulder to heavy set jaw, with no neck in between. Dark curly chest hair poked out from above a pink silk leotard, his hairy forearms hanging on either side of a pale pink tutu. He sat down across the aisle from Jim and placed his lunch pack on his knee, guarding it with carpeted knuckles. The schoolboys behind sniggered.

"He must be queer," one whispered.

"Oi! Fairy-"

The words bounced off the man's hairy back and he made no movement, but Jim could see his glistening eye.

"You ignoring us?" asked the first. "What you wearing that stuff for? You mental or what?"

Jim looked over his shoulder at the boys and the boys looked back.

"Here mister, lend us your hat so we can throw up in it," said the second boy to Jim, and they both guffawed.

Jim looked back to the huge man and down to the plastic pack on his knee. Spaghetti in tomato sauce. Probably last night's leftovers. A flask of beverage. He slipped his hand across the aisle and touched the man's hand. The man's eye continued to glisten, but he didn't take his gaze off the view ahead. His sausage-like fingers flinched and released their grip, letting Jim take the container in the palm of his hand.

Jim stood up and flipped the lid off the spaghetti. The boys looked up at him, their eyes round with anticipation. Then he took off his bowler hat, tipped the contents into it and dumped it on the nearest boy's head.

Spaghetti dripped onto the kid's shoulders and both boys sat in shocked silence. Jim unscrewed the flask and poured strawberry milkshake over the second boy's head.

The boys jumped up and fled the bus. As it took off with a hiss of exhaust, they ran behind, yelling. Jim watched his bowler hat hit the back window, smearing the glass with orange spaghetti. The huge man still had his eyes fixed ahead. Jim reached into his jeans pocket and extracted a five pound note. Then he leaned across the aisle and pushed it into the man's balled up fist.

Jim.

He stood up and zigzagged to the front of the bus, preparing to get off. As he waited, holding onto the hand rail above, his eyes moved upwards to the baggage rack where a little old man was half-awake, curled among the luggage.

The little man raised his head a fraction and looked from Jim's feet up to his head. He pulled his skinny knees closer to his chest and plumped up his bag-pillow with a bony knuckle.

Jim glanced at the bus driver, who appeared not to have noticed a thing. The other passengers on the bus continued talking, reading, daydreaming. Jim looked back to the skinny little man and noticed his dirty duffel coat, the stuffing coming through the seams and the toggles hanging by threads.

As the bus started to slow, Jim lifted the flap of his shoulder bag up and brought out a chorizo and melted cheese sandwich. He ripped it in half. In quarters. Then he raised his hand, with a piece between finger and thumb, and tossed it into the baggage rack. The little old man caught it in his open mouth. The bus slowed, slowed and stopped. Jim got off at his stop.

Homeostasis

When I awoke from my hibernation after the longest winter my soul has ever known, I found myself floating in a deep pool. Although my body drifted free on the surface and I had all the room I wanted to stretch my limbs, my neck and shoulders remained tensed. My muscles stayed clamped as though I were confined in the narrow space of a bathtub, rather than in the spacious pool. As my body rotated in the water, I could see bushes of deadly nightshade hanging over the edge of the pool, their purple heads oriented in a way that sent intoxicating perfume over me. Belladonna; a philtre of death.

The scent diffused the tension in my body and I felt myself succumb to the overpowering aroma. My multifidus loosened its bindweed-like grip from my spine and I sailed, detached, across the pool. Each muscle unleashed its store of lactic acid and I sensed my body melt into the cool water. I could feel myself disintegrate limb by limb, vertebra by vertebra, atom by atom and reform in the water.

I craned my neck. Looking down the length of my body, I noticed I was naked. My pale body looked stark against the dark pool.

But my Y had gone. Where the fork converged as one, now there was two. Another X. I had regressed to a state in which I had existed as part of another pool in another time; an amniotic former life, before I had become endowed with all that made me who I am. And now, as I looked at my new pubic mound, the hair ebbing and flowing on a rounded surface, I realised that who I had been was now gone. I had become a woman.

The water lapped between my legs and a new, warm sensation overcame me as I felt a warm suction. The current created entered my body and was gently expelled in pockets of air. My ears received the acute sound of this underwater transaction and I listened to the friendly murmurs of my being that soothed my stasis.

A soft pop announced the expulsion of a symbiotic tissue from my body. I saw a red, anemone-like creature bobbing in the wake I had created by raising my body. I touched the tiny thing and watched the red membrane fall away, leaving a peach-coloured prawn in the water. When I reached for it, it moved on the drift. Slowly, I slipped my hand under it and closed my fingers around it, to trap it. The curled, fleshy organism was exactly the colour of my hand.

I brought it to my mouth, dropped it in and swallowed.

A tiny bump descended through my body, radiating a soft light that I imagined to be a chakra. It passed between my breasts and along my stomach to below my navel and glowed rainbow bright as it reached its final stop, deep in the core of me. My Y had returned and the cycle was complete.

Where there had been belladonna before, now I saw orchids growing at the side of the pool. White orchids. The poison for me had gone and I knew the new scent caused me no harm. I put my hand on the side of the pool and prepared to enter the world, safe at last.

The Beach out of Reach

The sea is at low tide, the muddy sands covered in worm casts. You're walking along by yourself, and you see three figures far on the horizon by the distant water's edge. You try to catch up, but you can't. You wonder why you're having trouble walking; you look down and realise why. You're a swan.

You're in the wrong place; you shouldn't be at the beach. You take off, tucking your legs under you. You fly across the wide sands, but still the water stays out of reach and the figures stay the same distance away.

You feel empty.

***

As you fly towards the figures, you see that they are holidaymakers; two men and a woman. They're not what you expected. They present a happy façade but you see that it is shallow, like the distance tide. You're disappointed.

You sail on by, gliding with your wings stretched wide. The water that you thought was a sea is a pond. A dozen swans swim across the dark surface, between lilies. They are not swans like you. They are white like you, but they content themselves eating algae and preening their feathers. Nothing is like you.

You fly on.

***

You swoop lower. There is another pond. The water is dark like before, but the swans are fewer. Half a dozen skirt the muddy banks and a few take off like you, but not in the same direction.

It's not the right place.

***

There are four swans in the next pond. You fly close to the water's edge this time. The pool is stagnant. Algae grows on the waveless surface. It's not what you're looking for.

You turn upwards.

***

You skim the cool surface of a new pond, your feet creating waves. There are only two swans this time; it's more your home. The end is coming.

But not yet.

***

You see a small pond surrounded by trees and dip down into it, settling your wings by your side, legs tucked under. There are no other swans here. You are floating by yourself among lilies. You have achieved your goal. The emptiness of the pool is filled by the happiness in your heart.

All is well.

***

The pond drains away. The lilies rot into a soggy mass. Worms feed on the remains and muddy sands form. You are back on the beach where you first started. The figures are on the horizon. The water is out of reach.

Other books by Leilanie Stewart

The Fairy Lights: The ghost of Christmas that never was

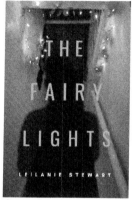

When Aisling moves into an old, Edwardian house in the university area of Stranmillis, Belfast, she soon discovers that her student digs are haunted. The house, bought by her grandfather decades ago, is also home to a spirit known by the nickname Jimbo.

As yuletide approaches, and Aisling's Christmas fairy lights attract mischief from Jimbo, she seeks to find out more about the restless entity. With the help of a local psychic and friends from her History with Irish course, Aisling uncovers dark, buried truths. What is the connection with Friar's Bush Graveyard just around the corner? What does Jimbo's dusty book of the Oak King and Holly King, hidden in the attic, have to reveal? What will Aisling's journey into the darkness of the spirit world reveal about Jimbo – and herself?

The Blue Man: A haunted friendship across the decades

Chill with a Book Premier Readers' Award and Book of the Month winner, February 2023

Two best friends. An urban legend. A sinister curse.

Twenty years ago, horror loving Sabrina told her best friend, Megan, the terrifying Irish folk tale of the Blue Man, who sold his soul to the Devil in vengeance against a personal injustice. What should have been the best summer of their schooldays turned into a waking nightmare, as the Blue Man came to haunt Megan. Sabrina, helpless to save Megan from a path of self-destruction and substance abuse as she sought refuge from the terror, left Belfast for a new life in Liverpool.

Twenty years later, the former friends reunited thinking they had escaped the horrors of the past. Both were pregnant for the first time. Both had lived elsewhere and moved back to their hometown, Belfast. Both were wrong about the sinister reality of the Blue Man, as the trauma of their school days caught up to them – and their families.

Why did the Blue Man terrorise Megan? Was there more to the man behind the urban legend? Was their friendship – and mental health – strong enough to overcome a twenty year curse?

The Buddha's Bone: A dark psychological journey to find light

Death

Kimberly Thatcher wasn't an English teacher. She wasn't a poet. She wasn't an adventurer. Now she wasn't even a fiancée. But when one of her fellow non-Japanese colleagues tried to make her a victim, she said no.

Cremation

In Japan on a one-year teaching contract at a private English language school, and with her troubled relationship far behind her in London, Kimberly set out to make new friends. She would soon discover the darker side of travelling alone – and people's true intentions.

Rebirth

As she came to question the nature of all those around her – and herself – Kimberly was forced to embark on a soul-searching journey into emptiness. What came next after you looked into the abyss? Could Kimberly overcome the trauma – of sexual assault and pregnancy loss – blocking her path to personal enlightenment along the way, and forge a new identity in a journey of-

Death. Cremation. Rebirth.

Gods of Avalon Road

London, present day.

Kerry Teare and her university friend Gavin move to London to work for the enigmatic Oliver Doncaster. Their devious new employer lures them into an arcane occult ritual involving a Golden Horse idol.

Britannia, AD 47.

Aithne is the Barbarian Queen of the Tameses tribes. The Golden Warrior King she loves is known as Belenus. But are the mutterings of the Druids true: is he really the Celtic Sun God himself?

Worlds collide as Oliver's pagan ritual on Mayday summons gods from the Celtic Otherworld of Avalon. Kerry is forced to confront the supernatural deities and corrupt mortals trying to control her life and threatening her very existence.

About the Author:

Leilanie Stewart is an author and poet from Belfast, Northern Ireland. She has written four novels, including award-winning ghost horror, The Blue Man, as well as three poetry collections. Her writing confronts the nature of self; her novels feature main characters on a dark psychological journey who have a crisis of identity and create a new sense of being. She began writing for publication while working as an English teacher in Japan, a career pathway that has influenced themes in her writing. Her former career as an Archaeologist has also inspired her writing and she has incorporated elements of archaeology and mythology into both her fiction and poetry.

In addition to promoting her own work, Leilanie runs Bindweed Magazine, a creative writing literary journal with her writer husband, Joseph Robert. Aside from publishing pursuits, Leilanie enjoys spending time with her husband and their lively literary lad, a voracious reader of sea monster books.

Acknowledgements

Acknowledgements are due to the editors of the following magazines, in which some of these stories first appeared: *Monomyth* (The London Plane, 2010); *Carillon* (The White Kaleidoscope, 2010); *Dark Gothic Resurrected Magazine* (Don't feed the Cats, 2010); *Sarasvati* (Arachnid of Life, 2011); *The Pygmy Giant* (Seven pets for seven years, 2011); *Wufniks* (Jim, 2011); *The Crazy Oik* (Elsie's Eternal Eden, 2012); *Ariadne's Thread* (Homeostasis, 2013); *Mad Swirl* (The Beach out of Reach, 2013); *Weirdyear* (Glen Abbot and the Green Man, 2014); *Pure Slush* (The art of something out of nothing, 2014); *Dark Gothic Resurrected Magazine* (Til Death do us Boneapart, 2017); *Inane Pure Slush Volume 14, May 2017* (Fear of the Mould, 2017); *Amethyst Review* (The existence of things inside wall spaces, 2018). Cover and internal image elements with thanks to Canva.

My books wouldn't be what they are without the help of many fabulous people that have given so much to my writing; so I'd like to give something back to all the following lovely folks:

Thank you to my hubby and editor, Joseph Robert, for the story feedback and polish, to Heather for the fantastic proofreading work on the final draft and to Ellen Collier for the beta-reader feedback on the finished collection.

I'm grateful to all the following for their support of my writing: Amy Jeffrey, Kendra Sneddon, Jeanne Bertille, Mary Louise Stewart, Janine Maxwell, Sharon Duffy, Sharon Bell, Edith Logue, Stacey Stewart, Alison Dowdell and Zeena. You guys are amazing.

I've also met some awesome fellow authors through the Instagram community –

Megan A. Dell
(www.meganadell.wixsite.com/meganadell)

Anastasia Arellano
(www.instagram.com/writeranastasia26)

Amanda Sheridan
(www.instagram.com/amandasheridanauthor)
(www.facebook.com/profile.php?id=1000638780225
30)

Isobel Reed
(www.isobelreed.net)

Please do check out their fabulous writing and follow them on social media.

Last, but not least, thanks to you for buying my book. Having readers keeps me motivated to write more stories, so just to let you know that I appreciate you taking the time to read and review my books. It means more than you know.